ACKNOWLEDGMENTS

To my family, who believed in me long before I wrote my first book.

Table of Contents

THE BEGINNING OF THE END

James drove down Rainier Avenue with the sunroof open and the bright Seattle sunshine beaming down on him and his new lady friend, Tanya. He met her over the weekend while club-hopping with his boys downtown. Each of them wanted to get on, but she walked right up to J and let him know she wasn't trying to holler at anyone else. Tanya was a red-bone with a long weave that fell to her mid-back. She had an itty bitty waist and a Coke-bottle shape. Her face was alright, but as long as the body was on point, that was irrelevant to James. She had a man, but no kids and no expectations, so he was willing to work with her.

James had been picking Tanya up from work every day this week; taking her out to eat, spending a couple of hours at a local motel, and dropping her off just in time to snatch up his wife, Asaya, from her job.

On cue, his cell phone started to vibrate. He looked at the screen and it said, "Mrs. Buchanan". He immediately hit the ignore button, sending her to voicemail. J made a mental note to change that contact info, because he surely did not put 'Mrs. Buchanan' in his phone. The phone rang again and once more, he denied the call. "Damn," he mumbled under his breath.

1

Looking at his watch, he noted it was only 3:30. His wife would not be off work until 5. He had told her time and time again not to contact him during business hours. James was a busy man and didn't have the time to spend sweet-talking his lady all day long. Besides, he thought it was a good idea that Asaya give him time to miss her.

James did love his wife, but somewhere along the way, he had lost interest. J had always loved a challenge and Asaya was never that—at least not with him. She fell head over heels for him from the gate and was not ashamed to show it. If he needed her, he called and she was always there. They could be in a room full of the flyest men in the town, yet she only had eyes for him. He heard that where she grew up, she was hard to get. She was the girl everybody wanted, but nobody could get their hands on. Apparently, he was a different story. At first, it was cute and he felt like other men were envious, but over time, it just got old and boring. James had rushed into asking Asaya to be his wife and start a family with him; but in hindsight, he realized that he was definitely caught up in the excitement of a new conquest, late night kicking it, lots of drinking and recreational drugs. By the time he came up for air, they lived together; she was pregnant, planning a wedding, and he'd had a change of heart. He loved Asaya and did not want to disappoint her, but J realized that he was still young and fly and that he could have any and every woman he wanted. He had reasoned with himself, *why limit yourself to just one?* He'd never had to settle for a mediocre woman and to him that is just what Asaya had become; average, run-of-the-mill. The cleavage-revealing tops that turned him on when he met her had been swapped for conservative outfits that left everything to the imagination. He had complained that no other man should see her breasts because she was his and she did not even put up a fight. She just changed her wardrobe. After the baby, the sexy body that J had salivated over transformed, too. Asaya was not obese, but she certainly did not have the body of a model that J was accustomed to. In his opinion, she could stand to lose a good fifty pounds. She had started working out and eating right a few months back, so she had shed about twenty pounds, but still had a long way to go. Patience was not something James had a lot of, so he was not waiting around for her to get it together.

Asaya listened as her husband's voicemail picked up again on the first ring. She believed he was ignoring her calls on purpose. She suspected James would tell her that his phone was dead, or on silent because he had a meeting. She glanced around the break room and saw people talking on their phones. Everyone seemed to be smiling or laughing. It dawned on her that she had not done that in a long time. She took one last peek at her phone, hoping for a missed call or text, but there was nothing. Slowly exiting the breakroom, she bypassed the elevator and entered the stairwell to make her way back up to the third floor.

Back at her desk, Asaya could barely focus on work. She sat there lost in her thoughts, reflecting on her life. When she met J, things started out beautifully. They did not have kids, so they were able to kick it every night of the week. Sometimes, Asaya would be at work on a couple of hours of sleep like it was nothing, only to do the same thing the next day. James wanted his girl to be with him wherever he was and made sure everyone knew she was his.

Asaya was tall and pretty with a nice body and the smoothest, ebony-colored skin you had ever seen. She had soft, wavy shoulder-length hair that made you think she was from some exotic place, other than the South End of Seattle. Her slanted eyes were the color of coal and they intrigued every man or woman she happened to steal a glance at.

James was considered eye candy by every woman he met. He was 6'0", with skin the color of 24-karat gold, the body of a god and a low cut, jet-black Caesar with deep waves. Asaya and J couldn't help but make a scene wherever they showed up together. The two were inseparable. Asaya was not interested in having kids, but James wanted her to have his and asked her to marry him. He even surprised her with an engagement ring just a few months into the relationship. Excited by the proposal from her new love interest, Asaya eagerly agreed.

As soon as she got pregnant, everything changed. James started to leave her home alone while he went out, and suddenly was not ready for marriage. The only reason they tied the knot when she was six months pregnant was that he was trying to make up for stepping out again. After the quickie backyard wedding, there was no honeymoon or celebration. They just returned home to a repeat of the same problems that had been plaguing their union. Asaya jumped when her co-worker called her name. Back to work...

James' eyes popped open and he sat straight up, looking around. His eyes focused on the clock next to the bed in the dingy hotel room. It was 5:45 pm. "Oh, shit!" he shouted. "Tanya," James ordered, "get yo' ass up!" He jumped up and started frantically throwing on his clothes while urging her to do the same. James was late to pick up Asaya from work. More importantly, Little J was still at daycare and the center closed at 6:00. He was dressed and ready to go within seconds. He spun around, only to see Tanya taking her sweet time. J grabbed his keys, ran out of the room, jumped in the gold Nissan Altima and drove off, leaving her standing there with her mouth hanging open.

J had never been late to pick up his son before and felt guilty imagining his boy sitting there, the last kid, waiting on his tardy parent. He punched the gas to the floor, dipping in and out of traffic to get to his mini-me. When he pulled up to the center, it was 6:00 and he breathed a sigh of relief.

Asaya had been standing outside her job for over an hour. She had called James' phone repeatedly, to no avail. Co- workers walked by, giving her the same sympathetic look they gave her every day. Some offered rides, while others asked if she was alright, but she held her head high and declined any assistance.

Finally, her phone rang and she picked it up. "Damn, what the fuck you been blowing up my phone for?" James asked.

"You know why I'm calling… I been off work for an hour and once again, no ride!" she answered.

"I got caught up handling business and then had to rush and get my son." J retorted.

Asaya started to argue. "You use my car every day and I can't even get picked—" The phone hung up on her mid-sentence.

James' car was in the shop, because someone had keyed it while he was parked outside of a hotel downtown. He told Asaya that he was there on business. Although she was suspicious of his account, she was sick of his lies, so she did not even bother questioning him. Nevertheless, he felt his S Series Mercedes needed an entirely new paint job and rims after that fiasco. James did not ask to borrow his wife's car. He just said, "Give me the keys," one day and never gave them back. Ever since then, any plans or priorities she had were either cancelled or fell through, because she was officially on J's time now. As far as he was concerned, he made plans and she should fall in line. Either that, or get out of the way. As he told her repeatedly, there were a million women, who would love to be in her position and what she wouldn't do, the next woman would.

Asaya sat outside her job waiting to see her car bend the corner, but by 7:00 pm, she had resigned herself to the fact that it just was not happening. The daycare was less than two miles away, so her ride should have been there. Asaya had no choice but to start walking to the nearest bus stop and figure out how to get home. She thought about calling her mother, or even her cousin, but the situation was embarrassing. She was not in the mood to hear that she had yet to learn her lesson. She was going to have to figure this one out on her own.

Three bus transfers later, it was 9:30 and Asaya was finally at the transit center near her home. She tried James one more time. This time, he answered and told her he was already comfortable at home and could not pick her up. He advised her to get on the bus and come home. Uncontrollably, tears fell down her face.

"Hello? Hello? Oh, wow. Let me guess… you're crying about riding the bus home?" James let out a frustrated breath and hung up. Asaya wiped her face as the other pedestrians started to stare and put the phone back into her purse. By the time she walked up to the front of her house, it was 11:30 at night. She rummaged through her purse for her keys before realizing her husband had them. Asaya knocked on the door loudly, but got no answer. The next ten minutes were spent beating on the door and calling J's phone. She sat on the porch, crying for some time before walking off into the pitch-black night.

EXPECT THE UNEXPECTED

"Mommy? Mommy? Mooooommmmmmmmmyyyy?" His eyes were still closed, but James could hear Little J calling out for his mommy, like he did every morning. He listened as the boy climbed the stairs in search of his mother. When he had safely made it to the top, J rolled over to try to get a few more minutes of sleep. He was forced to cut his nap short when his little boy ran back downstairs crying because he could not find his mom.

"Asaya? I know you hear JJ looking for you!" J yelled. He listened for a moment, but heard nothing. There were no smart comments, no smacking of lips and no slamming of doors, just silence. He ran upstairs looking around, only to find the bed in the master bedroom in the exact same disarray he'd left it in last night. His wife would never allow the room to stay in that condition if she were home. James rushed downstairs to retrieve his phone. Altogether, he counted 31 missed calls and 26 text messages from 11:30 until about 2:00 this morning. "Shit!" he exclaimed, realizing he had fallen asleep after hanging up on Asaya last night. He called her phone, but it went to voicemail every time. J was starting to worry. He frantically dialed Mrs. Annette

Johnson, his mother-in-law. He was sure that was the only place she would have gone. Under normal circumstances, James would never dial that lady. Mrs. Johnson believed her daughter could do better and she was probably right.

"What?" the agitated woman asked when she finally picked up.

Hesitantly, James replied, "Um… Good morning, Mrs. Johnson. Can I please speak to your daughter?" There was silence on the line and Mrs. Johnson finally said in an exasperated voice,

"You know damn well Asaya ain't over here. What the hell is going on? Where the hell is my baby? I swear on my life, if you did anything—"

James cut her off. "I ain't done nothing to your daughter! She caught the bus home and when I woke up, she was not here."

Mrs. Johnson grilled her son-in-law for all the details of the night, inquiring about why her daughter was on the bus, why she did not have a house key, what the reason was for her being left at work, where her grandbaby was and so on, until James finally ended the call. He told Mrs. Johnson he was going to call Asaya's job and some of her friends to try to track her down.

Mrs. Johnson anxiously wrung her hands after hanging

up the phone with her 'no-good ass' son-in-law. She knew he was all wrong for her only daughter. It seemed he had started out as Prince Charming and turned into a frog. If it were not for her grandson, Little J, she would have had one of her sons take him out of the game a long time ago. She dialed her daughter's cell phone number, only to get voicemail. "Hey baby, it's Mom. I'm really worried about you. Even if you just want to get away from that asshole of a husband you got, just let me know you're safe, okay?" After leaving a message, Asaya's mom started to go down the list of cousins, calling and asking if her child was at anyone's house. With every denial, Mrs. Johnson became more concerned that something horrible had become of her baby girl.

After hanging up with his mother-in-law, James looked at the time and saw that it was still too early for his wife to have arrived at work, so he racked his brain thinking of which friends of hers he should call. It dawned on James that he did not even know who Asaya knew or where to start the search for her. He'd stopped caring about where she went and who she was around a while ago, so all he could do was wait until 9:00 for her to arrive at work.

James turned on the television and started watching morning cartoons with his son. As he watched Little J smile and laugh at his favorite characters, he could not help but dread finally reaching his girl. He knew she was going to rain on their parade. Startled by the sound of his text message alert, J snatched his phone, just knowing it would be Asaya sending some text about how she had to sit out in the cold for hours and slept outside and so on. To his surprise, it was actually Tanya, cussing him out about leaving her at the room with no way home yesterday. He did not even read the whole message. He didn't feel he owed her any explanations. It was after 9:30 and Asaya was sure to be at the office by now. He knew she was a square, so she was guaranteed to make it to the slave ship on time every single day.

"Premier Finance and Accounting," the receptionist answered.

"Can I please speak with Asaya Buchanan?" James responded irritably.

"I'm sorry, sir, she is not in today." He hung up the phone, wondering where the hell she was. *Leave it to her to fuck his day off!* J was already behind schedule, there was a lot on his plate. First, there was getting his son to daycare, then meeting his partner, Rey, to discuss some upcoming business moves at the office. The plan was that Rey would be out of town for the next couple of weeks and planned to leave the handling of their joint venture to J.

James Buchanan and Reyhan Lucas had been best friends damn near all of their lives. They grew up together in the hood and most anything they got involved in, whether business or pleasure, was a partnership. If J needed to put money away for safekeeping, he gave it to Rey and vice versa. Whenever there was beef in the streets, J was the only person Rey would dial. If one of them were locked up or out of town with a little work piece, the other would look out and make sure his family was good until his return.

Unlike J, Rey did not have a wife and kid. For the most part, he had always been single. Growing up, James was loud, outspoken, and liked attention, both good and bad. Rey was more laid back. He came from a small family with both parents and a little sister. When he grew up and got his chips right, he made sure they were well taken care of. Hurting anybody that did not deserve it was not his forte. For that reason, he did not wife any of the females that attempted to lock him down or make random babies. When he settled down, it would be with his lady for life and his offspring would grow up just like he did—in a traditional family. Their conflicting lifestyles were the only point of contention between the two homeboys.

Rey was always on J's back about how he treated his

wife, but he was not some Good Samaritan out to save all the mistreated women in the world. He had known Asaya all of his life as well. As a matter of fact, they were friends, even before he and James got acquainted. In the fifth grade, because of his good grades, he got accepted to The Lakeside School just outside of the hood, and it so happened that she had been placed in the same educational institution. They spent the next seven years in the same classrooms and even went to the University of Washington together for college.

Throughout their friendship, they had spent countless nights studying together or just hanging out. Asaya's parents loved Rey and trusted him with her life, and his family felt the same way about her. Rey knew Asaya was a good girl and up until she hooked up with his boy, J, she was his closest friend and confidante. No matter whom they were seeing, nothing changed between them. That was what led to the demise of most of their romantic relationships. Most women he met did not like the fact that he spent so much time with Asaya.

She rarely let a dude get the time of day and when she did, the new man would always say he was uncomfortable with her relationship with Rey. So naturally, it would go nowhere. That all changed when she met J. It was hard to figure out how Asaya hooked up with him, but Rey did his best to talk to J about changing the way he treated her. James knew his boy just felt sorry for Asaya, so most of the advice went in one ear and out the other. In the beginning, there was no problem with the bond between Asaya and Rey, but over time the relationship started to make J uncomfortable. Instead of demanding his girl end the friendship, he punished her by adding new female "friends" to his roster. He claimed they were purely platonic, but Asaya doubted it. Nevertheless, Rey went from being around her twenty-four seven, to sneaking in conversation when J pulled one of his disappearing acts. Rey did not like going behind his boy's back, but if it kept him from making Asaya's life miserable, it was just what he would have to do... for now.

Pulling up to No Holds Barred, the local strip club, J got out of the car. He rubbed his hands together in anticipation of his new moves and the sight of half-naked ladies dancing around while he shot the shit. Looking around the parking lot, he noticed Rey's car was already there. He was always Johnny-on-the-spot. If he had somewhere to be, he would be there on time or earlier than needed. Owning a spot like this was a complete mismatch for Rey, but it did make sense. He had his hand in any and every legal hustle he could. Although strip clubs were not his thing, he would definitely use it as a means to an end.

"What up, mane?" James said, as he sat down at the table.

"Not much. You know, just trying to make a dollar out of fifteen cents," replied Rey. The two men spent the next two hours going over the details of the day-to-day operations of the club, to make sure no stone was left unturned. J did know how to take care of things, but sometimes his personal life got in the way.

"So, how Saya feel about you being in here on the regular for a second?" Rey asked, as they were getting up to leave.

"Oh, I forgot to tell you. Her ass never made it home from work yesterday! I don't know where the hell she is!" J answered.

The revelation stopped Rey dead in his tracks. "Why you just now telling me?" he demanded, clearly upset about the situation. Although irritated by the fact that Rey thought he had a right to know anything about *his* wife, James went over all of the details that led up to her disappearance. He did not sugar coat the story the way he did when Mrs. Johnson interrogated him.

Rey pulled his phone out and scrolled through the call logs, looking for a missed call or text from Asaya, but found nothing. He called her and like everyone else, got voicemail.

This was not like her; nowhere to be found and no contact with anyone? She surely would have called him to ask for help if there were problems with James. Because of the history they shared, Rey had become the go-to guy for both his boy and Saya, as he called her since childhood, when there was trouble in paradise; and there was *always* trouble in paradise. It was a tough position to be in because he knew deep down; J loved his wife. He just needed to get his act together and learn how to treat her. Most of the time, he purposely refrained from saying anything that would convince Asaya to leave. On the other hand, she was like family and he hated to see her always hurt and sad. When J disappeared from time to time with one of his sidelines, Asaya would call on him for advice or just to vent. He had promised her repeatedly that things would get better with time. He never let her know that he sounded a lot more confident about the potential in her relationship than he truly felt. Stevie Wonder could see that Asaya was wasting her time with J. The longer they stayed together, the worse it got for her. She had always been meticulous about the way she looked, dressed, and carried herself. But after four years with James, she had packed on extra pounds and started to wear inconspicuous clothing to hide her body. It seemed like the light Rey used to see in her had dimmed. Friends from grade school and college would often ask about her, because she had not been in contact in months and in some cases, years. A look back on the recent changes in his friend made Rey even more distressed about what had become of her.

Throughout the day, Mrs. Johnson and Rey stayed in contact with one another. They had still been unable to locate Asaya. Sometime around noon, James had stopped answering his phone He felt that Asaya had done this on purpose to get some attention and he'd had enough. Tanya was happy to hear from him after all of the bitter text messages she had sent. He picked her up from work early and they spent all day in a room together. To make up for leaving her yesterday, he copped a luxury suite at the DoubleTree Hotel. Her appreciation was a welcome distraction from the problems at home.

Rey, on the other hand, could not focus on anything throughout the day with Saya unaccounted for. He spent most of the day with her mom, helping and comforting her as best he could. It was a good thing everything was in line for him to leave tomorrow, because there was no way he could even think straight right now. He kept thinking that he had to find Asaya before his flight left in the morning.

Mrs. Johnson had agreed to pick her grandson up from

school today and keep him overnight. She expected to have news from her daughter by the time she returned that evening, but there was no word from anyone. Annette became more frantic and finally called the police. As expected, she got the spiel about how Asaya had to be gone for forty-eight hours, before an official missing person's report could be filed. However, Officer Williams did take down some information and said he would start looking into it. He, too, was upset to learn about Asaya's absence. They had lived on the same block throughout their adolescence. He had been called out a couple of times when James Buchanan had lost his temper and punched holes in the walls. J and Asaya's union was a mystery to him. They just did not match and his opinion was that she was too good for that guy. Growing up, every boy in the neighborhood wanted to make her his girl, but she would turn down every advance, including those from the future Officer Marquis Williams. He pursued her up until she met James and fell off the map. But even before that, he could not get close to her because her so-called best friend, Reyhan Lucas was always around cock-blocking. They claimed the situation was purely platonic, but it was hard to tell by the way he chased any other male away like a guard dog.

19

LIFE GOES ON

It had been three days since Asaya pulled this disappearing act and James was sick and tired of stressing about her whereabouts. As his mother used to say, "One monkey don't stop no show." During the daytime hours, while Little J was at daycare, J handled his business and ended each day with some sexual therapy with his new bottom bitch, Tanya. After Tanya found out what happened with wifey, she wasted no time getting rid of the square she was shacked up with, in hopes of taking Asaya's place. She had even started spending most of her time back at The Buchanan Compound, as J liked to call it. At first, he was skeptical about bringing another woman back to the home front. In all the years of doing dirt, he had never taken it that far. But the way James saw it, Asaya forfeited her position and he owed her nothing at this point.

With the money he was saving by not taking Tanya out every day and splurging on rooms, he was sure to be in position to finally invest in the soul food restaurant, The Silver Spoon, he and his cousin, William, had always dreamed of opening. J did not really get down in the kitchen, but nobody could cook better than Will. An establishment by the same name had already existed back in the day. All of the families in the hood would eat there after church on Sunday. They had the best ethnic cuisine in town. Large corporations were buying up the area where The Silver Spoon was located and family-owned businesses were being pushed out. Unfortunately, the owners of the eatery had leased the property for decades instead of buying it. So when the owner decided to sell to the highest bidder, the doors were closed. They could not afford another location, so they were forced to shut down for good.

William knew almost since birth that culinary arts was his calling, so while everyone else mourned the loss of the historical landmark, he had the wherewithal to take action to ensure he could revive it in the future. He got the money from James to purchase all of their classic furnishings and refurbished them, everything from the tables and chairs to the paintings on the wall. He also obtained ownership of the trademarked name, The Silver Spoon. Most importantly, he bought the rights to the treasured recipes and spent years 7perfecting them and adding many of his own. With James' business sense and his culinary excellence, this venture was sure to be a success.

The final piece of the puzzle was the location. After years of searching, they had finally settled on an Old

Pancake House building that had been vacant for years. The property was pretty run down, so they got it for pennies on the dollar. It was in need of some serious remodeling and with all the distractions in James' life, the process was slow. Will did not have the funds to pay for the business, but had the clean record so naturally, the property was placed under his name. J had the money and agreed to finance the project and upgrade it for fifty percent of all future profits. It was a solid move, because the two men had grown up more like siblings than cousins. Will was one of the few people J could always depend on. The only problem with doing business with family was false expectations. Will wanted the restaurant fixed up and open like yesterday, but J wanted to take his time and make sure it would not hurt him financially.

With the legalization of marijuana, J's illegal grow operation had turned into a legitimate business and he was able to invest in a real facility and employees. This meant he did not have to do all of the work by himself any longer and his income had quadrupled. But the overhead was expensive and he had to be sure he was sitting on a nice stack before throwing a couple hundred racks into The Silver Spoon. He and Will had nearly come to blows on many occasions because Will perceived J to be dragging his feet. Will thought that if it were J's dream, the spot would have been up and running in record time. But, since J was the money man, Will was on his schedule.

The way James saw it, a man's job is to get out and make it happen financially, and a woman's job is to support him in every way and keep his castle running like a well-oiled machine.

With Asaya missing in action, Jay needed someone to fulfill her duties and Tanya was his best candidate. Asaya knew what was expected and made sure she stayed on top on it. The house was always clean, laundry folded, breakfast and dinner on the table, whether he was there to eat it or not. He never had to chastise her about how to be a good housewife. If nothing else, she got that right.

He wanted Tanya to pick up where Asaya left off, but that was a tall order. Tanya was only good at two things, looking her best and sex. She did what she could to keep the house a little organized, but James still had to do some housework when he got home. Tanya could not cook to save her life. James could do alright in the kitchen, but had not needed to in years, thanks to his wife. Nowadays, he found himself making meals or ordering out. He had also brought in a maid a few days a week to keep the house in order. He was disappointed with Tanya's contribution to the household duties, but what she lacked in cooking and cleaning, she made up for in sexiness.

J did not miss a beat when Asaya cut out. His baby boy was another story. All this time, James had been telling Asaya if she left, her son would not even notice, but that couldn't be further from the truth. Every morning and night, Little J would cry for his mother for hours and would not go to sleep until he was completely drained. Tanya tried to comfort him on a couple occasions, but he wanted absolutely nothing to do with his daddy's new side chick. If there was one thing J had to admit that he missed about Asaya, it was her mothering skills. He silently admitted to himself that maybe he missed her cooking and cleaning, too.

Yesterday, James and Mrs. Johnson were finally able to make a police report about Asaya, but there was no clue as to where she had run off to yet. People wondered why he was not worried that maybe she had been kidnapped, raped or killed. He explained to anyone who would listen that Asaya would do anything to get some attention. Deep inside, he and everyone else knew the real reason she had left was him. Over the past couple of days, he kept finding himself reflecting on their relationship and the way he had treated her. Although he would never admit it, he did not blame her for leaving. It had been years since he saw a smile on her face and he knew he was responsible for that. He tried to pinpoint exactly when he turned into such a callous husband. He could not think of anything she had done to him to cause the disdain he felt for her. *Maybe it's me*, he thought. He just wanted to be able to do whatever he felt like doing with no questions or problems and here Asaya was, always questioning him or having a problem with *something*.

"Hey, J, I finished cleaning the bar and I'm headed home," the cute little bartender at No Holds Barred announced, snapping him from his guilt-ridden thoughts.

"Thank you, Carissa. Get home safely," he replied. She stopped and stared at him expectantly for a few seconds. James knew exactly what she was waiting for. The first day he was running the bar, he had offered her a ride home and she accepted. The ride home never happened. Instead, it turned into an all-nighter in the back office of the club and she wanted a repeat performance. Bringing her into Rey's office had been a big mistake. Rey would be pissed if he knew his boy was fraternizing with the help. He would be irate to know that anybody other than J had been inside his office. Rey could count the people he trusted on one hand and they did not include his employees. Drama was out of the question, especially when it came to making a profit. He had trusted James to handle things like he would in his absence and this was not a good look. After receiving no response from J, Carissa turned around and stormed out of the club, slamming the door behind her. James locked up and turned on the security system before jumping into Asaya's car to go pick up Little J from Mrs. Johnson.

His mother-in-law did not agree with his actions, but she would not hesitate to watch her grandson, no matter what time he was dropped off. Besides, she would rather have him with her than gallivanting around town, doing *Lord knows what* with his irresponsible dad. J was tired and not in the mood for the disapproving looks and comments he was sure to receive from his wife's mother, when he showed up to get his son at three o'clock in the morning.

Pulling up to the modest light brown rambler with the meticulously manicured lawn, James had a feeling of dread, because he could see Mrs. Johnson sitting at the kitchen table through the window. She was wide-awake and ready to look down her nose at him like he had shit on his face. But it was not always this way. In the beginning, both Walter and Annette Johnson loved James like he was one of their very own children. He and Mr. Johnson would hang out all weekend, barbecuing and drinking together. James really enjoyed hearing about his father-in-law's younger days growing up in Los Angeles, California. His father had not really been there for him when he was a youngster, so it felt good to have that type of relationship with an older man. Asaya's parents did not even bat an eyelash when her new boyfriend dropped to one knee in front of the entire family and asked her to marry him just three months into the relationship. They were pretty good at reading people and agreed that he was a standup guy.

Asaya got pregnant six months after the proposal and the shit hit the fan. James was not sure he was a one-woman man any longer. He also did not know if he was ready to have a family and take care of kids yet. He even insisted that she abort the baby, but she refused. When his fiancée was three months pregnant, he decided he needed to be out of town for a few months to take care of some business. There was no warning or preparation. Suddenly, Asaya was pregnant and alone. She kept a good job, so money was not a problem. About two weeks after James' departure, Mr. Johnson suddenly died from heart complications. J tried to make it back for the funeral, but got caught up and missed it. From that point on, Mrs. Johnson knew he was no good for her daughter. He finally came back when Asaya was about six months along, but by that time, the damage to the relationships he had with her and her relatives had been done. Whatever spark the young couple had in the beginning had been doused with cold water.

The front door swung open and Mama Johnson stood there with her hand on her hip. "Are you just going to sit there all night—I mean all morning?" she asked sarcastically.

"No, ma'am," he replied as he exited the car. He brushed past her into the house to retrieve his baby boy. James looked down at his son, sleeping so peacefully on his grandmother's couch. His jet-black curly hair was shiny and he smelled fresh like baby lotion. Mrs. Johnson always took good care of Little J at her house. She would make sure he was fed, bathed, clothed and comfortable. She would hold him tight until he fell asleep in her arms. In fact, the only time he was not crying lately was when his granny had him.

James slowly packed up his son's things, careful not to disturb his peaceful slumber. Annette noticed his hesitation and put her hand on top of his to stop him from loading the diaper bag. "Listen, son," she started, "the baby is fast asleep. Ain't no need to wake him this late at night. Let him rest and take him home in the morning." Usually James would object, but between the late nights at the club, followed by late nights at the house with Tanya

28

and making sure he spent time with his son, he was too tired to argue.

"Yes, ma'am," he said, in response to her request. But he was taken aback by the fact that Mrs. Johnson had just referred to him as "son". She had not used that word in regards to him since the beginning of his and Asaya's relationship. Since then, he had been called everything but a son of God. But the truth of the matter was, Annette felt kind of sorry for the young man. She knew he was a good father to her grandchild, but made poor decisions and she blamed James' deadbeat mother for part of that. Although he did his best to remain nonchalant about it, she could tell he was really upset and concerned about his wife. James stood up and started to put his jacket on when once again, he was stopped by his mother-in-law. *Damn, what the hell could possibly be the problem now?* he thought.

"It's late and I can tell you been drinking. I think it would be best if you stay here with your son 'til morning—"

James interrupted her, saying, "But I gotta get back to the house to take care of something."

Annette was not having it and told him, "Whatever needs to be handled can wait a few hours. Now come to the kitchen table, I'm going to heat up some leftovers from dinner for you and give you something *non-alcoholic* to drink!" He sat down at the table, knowing he had lost this debate.

The leftover beef brisket and stir-fry vegetables were the first home-cooked meal J had eaten in days, but to him, it seemed more like months. Asaya had definitely learned her way around the kitchen from mom dukes. He finished his first plate so fast; Mrs. Johnson thought he must have been on the verge of starvation. Without asking, she piled another helping on his plate and he thanked her and dug in.

James was so engrossed in his food; he did not notice the tears streaming down Mrs. Johnson's face until he looked up to ask if there was any more brisket. Crying and emotions was definitely not J's area of expertise. He tried to stay as far away from sad women as possible. Whenever his wife was upset and emotional, he would exit the house as fast as he could, because he knew he couldn't provide the needed shoulder to cry on. But what could anybody expect from him? His mother was an abusive dope-head, and she would whoop his little ass, anywhere and everywhere she felt like he was acting out. He got beat in church, in the store, at birthday parties and at the park. Pick a location and you can best bet he felt the sting of his momma's hand there. The words "I love you" were not something that was thrown around in the Buchanan household, so he never really knew what situations to use them in. But that all changed with Little J. The only time he was emotional was with his son. He made sure he always expressed how much he loved the little guy and consoled him whenever he needed it. J would be sure his boy would not grow up the way he did.

"What's wrong, Mom?" he asked.

Mrs. Johnson abruptly said, "Nothing. Everything is fine." He knew she was lying. Never in the years he had been around this woman had he seen her drop a single tear.

He walked up to her, put his hands on her shoulders and pleaded, "Please, tell me what's wrong." He really expected her to make another denial, wipe her tears and pull it together. Instead, it was like the waterworks turned on. In between sobs and sniffles, all he could make out was that she had lost her husband and now her baby girl was missing. James had been at odds with this woman for years, but never really stopped to think about all she was going through. For the first time in his life, he held a crying woman and felt genuine feelings of empathy. As the tears welling in his eyes threatened to run down his cheek, he could not help but wonder what the fuck was happening to him.

THE KNOCKOFF HOUSEWIFE

James and Little J got in the gold Altima to head home just after dawn. He had not gotten a lot of sleep last night, but felt slightly refreshed after the time he spent with Asaya's mom. After her emotional breakdown, he had tucked her in to get some rest and washed the dishes she had used to prepare his late night meal.

Jay had then snuggled up next to his son and fell asleep to his light snoring and fresh fragrance. It was the best few hours of sleep he had in days. When he woke in the morning, he got Little J dressed and peeped in on Mrs. Johnson, after lightly knocking on her bedroom door. He was worried about leaving her alone in her condition, but when he opened the door, she was fully dressed with her hair done and smiling from ear-to-ear. It was as if the vulnerable situation he witnessed last night never occurred. She kissed her grandbaby, gave them both a hug and walked them to the door to say goodbye. If she wanted to pretend she was fine and forget about last night, he was cool with that. At least he would never have his own sensitive display come back to haunt him.

J pulled up to his house and got out of the car slowly. He knew that Tanya would be upset about the fact that he was just getting back and he really did not feel like making explanations to some random broad. Before he could turn the key and unlock the door, Tanya snatched the door open. She started to scream at him, "Where the fuck you been? You think you gone have me sitting here waiting for yo' ass like that stupid bitch did? You got me fucked up!"

James wanted to slap the taste out of her mouth for talking like that in front of his child, but instead he did what any responsible parent would do. He turned around and went right back to the car with his son, but not before noticing the stuffing from the couch all over the living room floor. This was the couch Asaya had spent all day shopping for just two weeks ago. He was seething with anger, but decided to drop his little guy off at daycare before attempting to deal with the situation. After arriving at the childcare center and ensuring that his kid was safely away from all the bullshit, J sped back toward his home to handle the belligerent bitch.

James was just about to pull up at his house when he got a phone call from the club. When he picked up the phone, his head of security, D-Lo, sounded panicked and out of breath. "Aye yo, J, you have to get down here right away, bro!"

"What's up? Is everything cool?" James inquired. D-Lo

would not discuss what was going on over the phone, but made it clear that J needed to be there immediately, so he turned around and headed toward the club as quickly as possible. When he arrived, the place was crawling with uniformed police officers and detectives. As soon as he stepped out of the car, the last person he wanted to see walked up to him. Officer Williams asked him if he was running the club. James cautiously said he was running it in the interim while the owner was out of town. He was careful not to say exactly who the owner was. Marquis let him know that there was an anonymous call regarding a break-in at the club and upon entry, law enforcement found several illegal automatic weapons throughout the premises. This could not be true. Rey would never be involved in illegal activity—at least not these days. Shady activity, yes, but never illegal. He went on to explain that the security system was disengaged and the front door was standing wide open when the cops got there. Nobody would be arrested until they got fingerprints off the weapons, but the club would be shut down indefinitely and possibly permanently. J mumbled under his breath, "This shit *cannot* be happening!" He had only been in charge for a few days and he had already gotten the spot shut down. His boy was going to have his head.

As the cops were finally leaving, a feeling of dread suddenly came over J. He ran through the front door of the club, almost tripping over the rug. He rushed past the restrooms and into the back office. The door was unlocked and J knew right then his worst fears had come true. He rushed to pull the huge Mona Lisa replica off the wall behind Rey's desk. He was so nervous; he had to try the safe combination twice. When he finally got it open, it was completely empty. James dropped to his knees with his head in his hands, hoping he could somehow will his friend's five hundred thousand dollars back where it belonged. But this was really happening. His best friend had trusted him and left his bread and butter in his hands.

He was solely responsible for losing the seed money Rey would use to open his black-owned grocery store. He had talked about this thing ever since the day James met him. Rey's grandfather spent his whole life working for one of the large chain supermarkets and investing any money he had into company stock. When he got sick a couple of years before retirement, he attempted to sell some of his shares back to get the money needed for his medical treatment. His employer found a clause in the contract that allowed them to steal what Mr. Lucas had worked so hard for from under him. Both of Rey's parents were public school teachers and could not afford the needs of his papa. So in the end, he passed and left nothing to his family. Since that day, Rey promised himself he was going to make sure the people from his hood actually owned something there, and were able to leave a legacy for their children and grandkids. J couldn't bring himself to tell Rey what happened. All he knew is he had to get it back and quick.

J sat there racking his brain to figure out what the hell happened at No Holds Barred. As far as he knew, the only people that even knew about the safe in the office were he and Rey. He knew that guy would never tell a soul about the location of the stack. Then it dawned on him that Carissa had been in the office with him a couple of nights ago. He knew the rules about bringing employees back there, but she had convinced him to do a couple of lines with her. Combined with liquor and her barely-there clothing, it made him lose both his inhibitions and his good judgment. He was headed to the back to lock up the night's profits, and she started flirting and talking. He didn't remember what the conversation was about, but could tell you exactly what she was wearing. In a rush to get down to the business at hand, he quickly deposited the funds into the safe when he thought she was not looking, but in hindsight he really could not be sure. The more he considered the suspects, the more Carissa looked the most viable. James pulled out his cell phone and scrolled through his contacts to find her number. After hitting send, he listened for the phone to ring, but only got a recording from T-Mobile, stating that the number was out of service. "Shit!" he yelled out. He ran to the file cabinet and pulled out her personnel file. Scanning the paperwork inside, he found her address and wrote it down.

Within a matter of seconds, he was in his car, using the GPS system to find the house. "Your location is on the left," instructed Siri. James felt like crying as he surveyed the vacant lot at the location. He now knew Carissa had set him up, if that was even her name. How the hell was he going to explain this to Rey? And how could he possibly replace the money? There was a stack of about a hundred racks at the house, and he had an additional two hundred fifty thousand dollars in a safe deposit box at the bank his uncle ran. But that money was for his and Will's restaurant. There was absolutely no way he could use that as reimbursement. And what about the club? It was out of commission, so that was another loss his boy would take.

When James pulled up in front of his house early afternoon, he still had not contacted Rey to let him know what had gone down at the spot. He did plan to tell him, but could not find the right words, so he was taking his time. As he walked toward the front door, he suddenly remembered the problems from this morning with Tanya. He picked up his stride to get into the house to assess the damage she had done to his shit. He stepped into the foyer of the home and looked around the floor, noticing that the filling from the couch was no longer scattered about. As he went into the living room, he saw that the couch Asaya had bought recently had been replaced with a similar sofa. Before he could assess the quality of the new furniture, Tanya appeared at the kitchen entrance. She was clad in a skimpy maid uniform, and was holding a tray with steam rising from the hot meal she had prepared for him. As she approached him, she apologized repeatedly and begged his forgiveness. Usually if a chick had gotten beside herself the way Tanya did, she would be on the first thing smoking up out of his spot, but right now he needed her. Any time things went wrong in the streets, he would come home to Asaya and she would take care of him and nurse him back to health until things blew over. But she was gone to God knows where and Tanya was here ready and willing to please. He pushed his wife, No Holds Barred, and Reyhan Lucas out of his mind for now and focused on the moment.

"My friend called and told me what happened, baby.

I'm so sorry to hear about it," murmured Tanya.

Damn, the streets were already talking. This town is way too damn small! J thought. He let her know it was something he did not want to discuss, and that she better not be talking about it with anybody else either. Tanya assured her new man that she would do anything to please him and proceeded to do just that.

After he finished the meal that he suspected she bought instead of cooked, she produced a blunt for him to smoke and turned on some soft music for him to relax. As she rocked back and forth sensually, James slowly drifted into an erect stupor and leaned back, ready to be pleasured. He watched her through barely open eyes as she dropped to her knees and unbuckled his jeans. She skillfully slid his pants and boxers down to his ankles, leaned in and starting gliding her tongue ring up and down his phallus. As James' eyes rolled back in his head, he thanked goodness Mrs. Johnson was picking Little J up from daycare. He was definitely going to need to sleep this one off. After enjoying the foreplay festivities on the brand new sofa, J swooped his lady friend into his arms and carried her up the stairs and into the master bedroom to start the main event.

By the time Tanya finished servicing J with one of her infamous marathon sex sessions, it was late in the evening and she knew that she had put it on him so good, it was impossible for him to keep his mind on any of his troubles. She had learned from an early age that she'd had a gift with the men. Shit, every pedophile ass, low budget, new daddy her momma brought home made that clear. Instead of bitching and wining about the abuse she had to endure, Tanya Ford used the experience to her advantage. She was an expert at using what she had to get what she wanted. She was not the prettiest girl around or even the smartest. But where she was from, if you just happened to be born light-skinned with light eyes, you got a head start on the competition. The fact that she had inherited her mother's wide hips, an itty-bitty waist, and the perkiest C cups made her a ten in the average man's mind. When she set her sights on a dude, no matter whose man it was, it was only a matter of time before she made him her own.

Tanya had done her homework and she knew all about J and his hustle. She had only been around a short time and she was already in the spot playing wifey. When she met up with her best friend, Jayla, they marveled at this new record T had set. She had lived with many men in the past and always had a sucka on standby, ready to pick her up any time one of these lames lost interest and decided she needed to vacate the premises. But J was certainly not one of those.

She had most definitely hooked one of the big fish in the pond this time. He was not at the top of the food chain like Reyhan Lucas, but he had ambition and potential and T could work with that. Besides, Rey's old uppity ass thought he was too good for the likes of her. He was the finest man she had ever laid her eyes on. He was six feet tall with skin the color of bronze and not one blemish on it. His features were chiseled and he reminded her of Idris Alba. His body was cut up from head to toe and you could tell he stayed away from drugs and alcohol; all the shit J loved.

She had tried numerous times to 'accidentally' bump into him wearing the sexiest clothes she had, giving him an up close and personal look at her *assets*. When he ignored her, she came back with a more conservative approach next time, but he still did not give her the time of day. Tanya was starting to wonder if he was gay or something. *But fuck him!* T had moved on to the next best thing and was living high on the hog nowadays.

Tanya was feeling like a queen and there was no way on earth she would ever let J's whack ass wife back into this castle.

As she looked down at her fine ass man, she vowed to herself that she would do whatever it took to secure her spot next to him forever. Come hell or high water, she would be the next and last Mrs. James Buchanan, the only one that mattered.

NEW BEGINNINGS

Annette Johnson stared down at her grandbaby as he slept peacefully across her lap. She had decided to keep him home from daycare for a few days, because of all the chaos going on with his parents. There had not been a day in the child's life that he had not gone to sleep and woke up next to his mom. That was the one stable thing in his life. No matter what stress and strife Asaya was going through, she did her best to maintain a sense of normalcy for her son. She was always making excuses about why James would be gone overnight or sometimes for days at a time. JJ reminded Annette so much of his grandpa, Walter. He was always in a good mood, no matter what was going on and he rarely made a fuss. His grandfather would fall in love if he were still here.

Mrs. Johnson was ecstatic when her son-in-law called yesterday evening and asked her if James Jr. could stay for a couple of weeks. He told her that he had a lot going on and needed to handle some business situations. The way J talked about his upcoming schedule made it sound like business as usual, but she knew better. The streets were already talking about what went down at No Holds Barred. Walter Jr. had shown up late last night to say hello to his mother and while he was there, he let her in on the scandalous details of the strip club heist. Normally, under such circumstances, she would fly into a panic and start calling Asaya, begging her to bring the baby and stay with her for safety reasons, but not this time. Her grandson was in her home for the next two weeks and she had finally found out that her baby girl was safe.

The night James had stayed over her house with the baby, Annette had cried herself to sleep, overwhelmed with worry about her daughter. Early that morning her cell phone was vibrating and it was from a private number. When she picked up the phone, she was pleasantly surprised to hear Asaya's voice. "Hi, Mom," her child said after she answered.

"Oh my Lord! Asaya?" she asked.

"Yes, Mom, it's me. Are you alone?" Asaya whispered, as if she did not want to be overheard.

Annette automatically changed her voice to mimic her daughter's secretive tone. "Kind of... Little J is in the living room asleep with his dad and I'm in the bedroom. Nobody can hear me. Baby, are you okay? Where are you? Do you need me to—"

Asaya cut her mother off. "Mom, I'm fine. I'm okay. Calm down, please." Mrs. Johnson relaxed a little and listened intently as her daughter explained the events that had taken place over the last four days.

Asaya let her mother know that being locked outside was the straw that broke the camel's back. She had been on the fence about leaving James for years; that night and the day that preceded it validated the feelings she had already had. Contrary to what her husband thought, Asaya knew exactly what was going on with James and Tanya, among all of the other women he was seeing. She had begun to see a counselor by the name of Tony Jackson a couple of months ago. Initially, Asaya hoped he would make the decision for her, telling her she needed to leave immediately. Instead, he had advised her not to make any rash moves and that she should not leave her relationship, unless she was sure she was done with it and was prepared mentally and financially. Through the therapy process, she stopped focusing on what James was doing wrong and put all of her energy into JJ and herself. Tony helped her to see that her husband had only done what she had allowed him to do to her, and that it was not logical to expect another person to respect you when you did not even show yourself the respect you deserve.

That realization was just what Asaya needed to motivate her to take off the fifty-plus extra pounds accumulated over the last few years. She used to be diligent about what went into her body and making sure she stayed active, but she had let being a mother and dealing with all of the difficulties of her relationship take precedence and it showed in her appearance. Her workout partners had been rejected so many times; they finally stopped calling to invite Asaya.

Mrs. Johnson listened intently as her daughter shared all of the painful experiences she had been forced to keep to herself in recent times. In the beginning, Asaya told her mom about everything that went down in her household. She quickly learned that was a bad idea. Her family turned against James and wanted her away from him, and he blamed her for causing the rift. Her siblings became distant because they no longer agreed with the choices she was making. Friends were downright disgusted that the woman they had known for so long would ever allow a man to treat her so horribly. They had grown tired of the excuses as to why she could never do anything with anyone other than James or James Jr. Eventually, Asaya learned to keep her business to herself and ended up isolated. She had pushed her family out of her life in order to protect her husband, although she never felt like the kind of married woman every little girl dreamed of growing up to become.

Hearing her only baby girl relay what she had gone

through was enough to bring Annette to tears. Following the stories that lead up to her disappearing, Asaya told her mother what she had been doing since then. A couple of months back, Tony had told her about a self-help boot camp called The Restoration Retreat, located in Hawaii. The camp was run by Tony's wife, Lisa, and would take place over a one-month period. When Asaya heard about it, she immediately knew she had to go, so she attempted to speak to James about signing up. He didn't even listen to the details before telling her they did not have money to waste on her "mental issues". He said he needed her there with their son and said there was no way he was going to babysit for a whole month. Asaya found it funny that when she had Little J, she was doing her job, but when J took his boy, it was babysitting.

The retreat began on Monday; the same day she was left at work. That night, after walking two miles in the middle of the night and getting a room at a nearby run-down Super 8 Motel, Asaya stayed up wishing she had participated in the camp. After much thought and tears, she decided there was no reason she could not do it. So, early in the morning, she called Tony and asked if it was possible for her to come, although she was late. He was excited to hear from her and after checking with his wife, agreed that she should still come. She followed that call by contacting her supervisor at work. Because everyone knew about what had been going on in the Buchanan household and due to her stellar work history, Ms. Leighton was more than happy to approve a leave of absence for the next three months. Asaya could finally put to use all of that paid time off she had saved for a family vacation that never happened. By noon, she had caught a cab to the mall and bought some new clothes, shoes, books, toiletries and a carry-on, made it to the airport and was ready to board the plane for the six-hour flight. "Now boarding flight 645 to Honolulu, Hawaii at gate 10-B," was announced over the intercom. Asaya took one last glance at her phone. She had turned on call rejection, sending all calls to voicemail after speaking with Tony this morning. James had tried calling and texted damn near a hundred times. This was something new. She guessed he must now know what it feels like to be left hanging. There were also missed calls from her mom, her brothers, and Rey. She held down the power button to turn off the phone before walking through the gate. She would be sure to let her family and her best friend know she was okay as soon as she arrived.

The flight was long, and the fact that Asaya started to be consumed with worry about what she had done, did not make it go by any faster. She pondered what people would think about her. She was sure they would assume she just up and left her son without even saying goodbye. She wondered if JJ would forget who she was and if James could take care of him as well as she did. She was curious as to whether he was going to bring any of his side chicks around Little J. About halfway through the flight, she decided that worrying was not going to help the situation. She knew she needed to do this. Asaya had thought this through more thoroughly than any decision she had ever made. She had certainly considered it more thoroughly than marrying and procreating with James Buchanan. If there was one thing she did trust about James, it was that he would never allow any harm to come to his son. JJ was his prized possession and absolutely nothing came before him. She asked the flight attendant for a shot of vodka to help her relax. Asaya drifted off to sleep and dreamed about tropical temperatures, blue water, white sandy beaches and most notably, a feeling of peace and happiness. She awoke as the plane was landing, just in time to look down at the beautiful island. Yes, she felt she had made the right decision. She would return to her life a stronger and better person.

Lisa Jackson walked up to greet Asaya as she exited the Honolulu International Airport. Asaya extended her right arm, but Lisa bypassed it and hugged her tightly as if they were long lost friends. She was surprised by the embrace, but it made her feel a lot more comfortable about being here. Lisa was a tall, brown-skinned woman. Her straight, jet black hair rested just below her shoulders. Asaya looked her up and down, but could not find a single hair out of place. Her burgundy romper was perfectly pressed, and looked like it belonged on her body. It looked like she had never eaten anything unhealthy and worked out every day. She carried herself like royalty, but something about her was warm and welcoming. Lisa signaled for the bellboy to come over and grab Asaya's bag then took her hand and led her to the waiting Town Car. The ride from the airport to the Hawaiian Princess Resort was about forty-five minutes. That gave the ladies time to get to know one another. It was obvious that Lisa knew what was going on with Asaya, but she did not address her in the 'poor girl' tone that her co-workers and everyone else did. It was more like she understood, but still had respect for the younger woman. Asaya felt she could let her guard down and open up more than she had in years. They talked about their families and careers on the way to the resort. By the time they arrived, she had shared more about her life than she had with anyone, outside of Reyhan Lucas.

When they stepped out of the car, Asaya was speechless at the sight of the place that would be her home for the next three months. She was given a tour of the premises and shown to her beachfront condo. As soon as she walked in, she sat her bags down and walked straight to the balcony to take in the view of the Pacific Ocean. Everything was perfect, from the extra plush queen-sized bed and the fully equipped kitchen, to the overstuffed lounge chair on the balcony overlooking the ocean. That spot was ideal for reading. She was grateful that Lisa had retired to her own room to give her time to take it all in and rest. That Tuesday night was used to catch up on the sleep Asaya had missed the day before. There was no tossing and turning like she did all night when at home. She sat on the balcony for about an hour reading the *1325 Buddhist Ways to Be Happy*. After a nightcap of the pineapple Cîroc she found in the refrigerator, Asaya did not even make it to the bathroom to wash up before collapsing on the bed and falling to sleep. The retreat had not even started for her, yet she already felt like a different woman.

Asaya woke up Wednesday morning lost and disoriented.

Everything had happened so quickly yesterday that it all

seemed like a dream. She sat up in the bed and looked around the room. For some reason, being there in the daytime made it more real. The shower was built to look as if you were outside washing in a waterfall. Once she got in, it was hard to pull herself away. Asaya walked back into her room to find that a light breakfast, consisting of a veggie omelet and whole wheat toast with fresh preserves had been served, and a schedule for the first four weeks of the boot camp had been left on her bedside table. "Group breakfast, individual therapy, exercise class, team building, hang gliding, zip-lining, movie night, snorkeling, surfing... sheesh!" she read aloud. The list went on and on. For a girl who had done nothing but primarily work and stay at the house with a kid for a handful of years, this seemed a bit ambitious. Asaya was skeptical about the hectic schedule, but promised herself she would get involved in every single activity, no matter how tired she got.

The trip looked like it would be a lot of hard work on paper, but in reality, everything they did was fun and rewarding. The first few days had been the best time of her life. There was no way she could ever regret this decision. During the individual therapy, she started to learn to forgive and treat herself better. In the group and teambuilding activities, Asaya met many women from different walks of life, all with their own issues. Some seemed to be worse than hers and others not, but she left the sessions feeling like maybe her life was not horrible after all. The only downside was missing her baby boy. Anytime those thoughts came, she continued to remind herself that it gets greater later.

Hearing her daughter recount her comings and goings of the past four days had made Annette smile. She believed that if anyone deserved to enjoy life and be happy, it was this young lady. She had always been the backbone of the family as a child and grew up to be the same for her own little family. Mrs. Johnson assured her daughter that Little J was okay with her and there was nothing to worry about. She relayed every little cute thing the boy had done over the past few days. The guilty feelings about leaving somewhat subsided when her mother let her know she was proud of her for taking the steps she needed to get her life back in order. She also encouraged Asaya to complete the process and to not be persuaded by anyone else's thoughts or comments about what she should do. Because Mrs. Johnson insisted no one interrupt the experience her baby girl was having, they agreed that it was best to keep her siblings and James in the dark about both the phone call and where she was. Annette would make sure her grandson was in good hands until his mommy returned. After they hung up, both ladies had breathed a sigh of relief.

MY BROTHER'S KEEPER

Rey stepped out of the elevator at the Embassy Suites in Lincoln City, Nebraska. As he walked over to the registration desk to check out, he could not help but smile at the realization that his lifelong dreams were finally coming to fruition. He had taken all of the necessary steps to ensure his stores would be a success. His attorney had called last week to let him know the name; For the People Food Market had been trademarked, and was his. He had been around the country in the last five days signing off on property deals for his farmland and production sites. Rey decided long ago that he would never be dependent on greedy growers and suppliers to keep his stores stocked. He would grow and create his own *FTP* products to sell alongside the national brands like Safeway and Kroger. That way, not only would he be employing people in the stores; there would also be farmers, production workers and salesmen. The possibilities were endless. He had bought up properties everywhere. Now he could produce any fruits, vegetables or organic products he needed. If it was not healthy, his people would not consume it. Not only would he retire his parents from their teaching careers; he would share the wealth with his entire community. Nebraska had the most land for growing anywhere in the United States and that is where he spent the majority of his budget, securing thousands of acres. All of the puzzle pieces were falling into place and the final steps were to fly into Hilo International Airport in Hawaii, to meet with the local businessmen there. He needed to close the deal on some tropical terrain where things like pineapples, papayas, bananas and mangos could sprout. When that final purchase was complete, he would take a week or two to relax on the beach, then return home and close on his first business location and sell No Holds Barred.

As Rey got into the waiting taxi, he pulled out his phone and dialed James' number for what felt like the hundredth time. He had been calling J and Saya the entire time he was gone to make sure she had returned home safely. Her phone continued to go to voicemail before ringing and his boy simply was not answering. But just when Rey thought James would once again let his call go unanswered, James picked up. "Hello?"

"Nigga, what you mean hello? You answering like you ain't see me calling a million times! Did you find Saya?" he countered.

"Nah, I ain't found her ass yet. But that's the least of our problems, bro." J continued.

"I'm not following you. What's good?" Rey demanded.

James came back with an attitudinal tone of voice. "I might as well just let you know straight up... the club got robbed and shut down a couple of days ago. Somebody got the cheese out the safe and that nigga, Marquis, swears he found some illegal guns and shit."

Rey damn near dropped the phone, stunned by the words he just heard. Immediately it seemed as if he had just been cracked in the temple with a mallet. His head was throbbing and his heart was racing.

"Rey? Rey? Are you still there? Man, my bad—" J started.

"Your bad, nigga? Your bad? What the fuck you mean, your bad? The money in the safe was for my building! How the fuck did somebody crack that shit? Did you do this? Where the fuck is my money?" Rey interrogated.

James was completely taken aback by the allegation. He knew the loss would be upsetting, but never did it cross his mind that Rey would think he actually had something to do with getting him.   "I ain't no fuckin' snake, dude. Somebody knew the combination and got us. That's it and that's all. We just gotta figure out a way to get that shit back," J responded.

"*We* ain't gotta do a muthafuckin' thing, boy! You better get my money back before I touch down!" Although James wanted to get hostile because of the way he was being spoken to, he bit his tongue because he knew exactly what Rey did to niggas in the streets that stepped on his toes. The more he tried to explain what happened, the angrier Rey became. He always knew his friend was a fuck-up, but this episode took the cake. Unable to stand the sound of James' voice, he hit the end button and tossed the phone. There was nothing James could say to make this okay.

His thoughts were interrupted by the ringing of his phone. He snatched it up off the seat, expecting it to be James calling back. To his astonishment, Asaya's name flashed across the screen. Rey's irate demeanor changed to concern at once. He answered the phone as quick as he could, afraid she would hang up before he heard her voice. "Saya?" he questioned.

"Hey Rey," she retorted so softly, it was almost inaudible. "Damn. How are you? Are you okay?" he asked.

"I'm fine... and I'm sorry for making everyone worry. I just needed to get out of my situation," Asaya explained.

"No, don't apologize to me. I'm just happy to hear from you. I was worried about you." She breathed a sigh of relief because she did not know what to expect and was glad Rey greeted her gently, instead of yelling at her and telling her how fucked up it was to have left her son. He listened intently as she relayed the same story she had told her mother about what happened and why she left. Rey was a little hurt to find out there were some things she did not trust him with; like the fact that she was in counseling and that she had jumped on a plane and left the state by herself. But, he of all people, understood why it was something she had to do. Most chicks would not have hung in there as long as she had. He respected her decision and gave the same heartfelt response that Mrs. Johnson had given. He cared about her deeply and wanted her to get back to the girl he used to know.

Asaya was surprised to find out that she was not the only one keeping secrets over the past few months. Rey communicated every detail of what he had accomplished toward For the People Food Market and left Asaya in awe. She knew he was more ambitious than anyone she knew and they were both convinced he would be wealthy and successful one day, but she was not aware that he was this close to making it happen. "I am so proud of you, Rey," Asaya gushed. She was always able to express exactly how she was feeling to him. There was never the worry about rejection, the fear of being told to quit simpering all the time if she was too caring, or the insult of being told she needed to learn how to act like a lady whenever she opposed something. It was easy to just be Asaya around Rey. He accepted her flaws and all, and kept it one hundred with her, always coming from a tender and loving place. Asaya knew she would never have another ally like Rey or the kind of chemistry they had together. He was not like any other guy she had ever met. His fondness for her was genuine and not just a ploy to see if he could get in her pants. Not once had he attempted to cross the invisible line and take advantage of Saya, even in her most vulnerable moments.

Knowing that his friend was cool, made Rey temporarily forget about the calamity that had just occurred at his business. When a thought about it did cross his mind, he made the determination right then and there that he was not going to tell her about any of it. He knew she had been in a miserable position for a long time and he wanted to get the old Saya back. The appreciation that Rey received from the contact with her put him in a good mood and he believed that one way or the other, he was going to find a way to make everything work out. They agreed that he would call Asaya as soon as he finished his meeting in Hilo in a couple of days and he would come see her before he left. She could not help feeling anxious about the visit. It would be fantastic to see a familiar face while she was so far away from home.

Rey spent the day in Hilo going from one conference to another, but by the end of the day, he had locked in everything he came there to get and was ready to take a break. The missing half a million dollars was a huge bump in his road to success. The only option was to do what Reyhan Lucas did best, and that was to hustle. When he returned to the mainland, he would need to first run through J's pockets and get back as much of his capital as he could. Next, it was time to hit the streets and collect on all debts he was owed. That would get him a little over halfway back to where he started and from that point, Rey would need to tap into some resources and see what shook. Of course, there was the family trust fund he set up specifically for his parents and his baby sister. That would be more than enough to cover the loss, but there was no way in hell he was ever touching those chips. He willed himself not to think about the No Holds Barred complications and ignored every call and text from James. As far as Rey was concerned, he needed actions, not explanations. Even more, it bothered him every time he looked at a missed call and it was not Asaya. If anybody could make him feel like everything would be fine, it was his best friend. He knew he said he would call tomorrow and they would discuss what time he would be in Oahu, but with business affairs wrapped up, Rey saw no reason not to unexpectedly pop up on her.

Rey called ahead and paid a small fee to change the flight. Instead of heading back home in a couple of weeks, he would divert his reservation to the Honolulu International Airport now, and then fly out of there in two weeks. He carried his bags through the Hilo Airport and jumped on the small plane that would carry him to his next destination. The flight was only about thirty-five minutes long and before Rey knew it, he was getting into a Lincoln Town Car to take the forty-five-minute trip from the airport to the Hawaiian Princess Resort. During the ride, he touched base with several associates to get some insight on what went down at his club. Through the grapevine, he found out about the details that James had left out. He knew that Carissa was thirsty, but she was a good look for the club, so he steered clear of her and warned his boy to do the same. Against every piece of advice and logic, J had brought this girl into the back office and lost everything Rey had there. This still did not explain the presence of the weapons the police found. To him, it did not make sense for Carissa to set him up just because she wanted to jack him. He would be sure to pay his boy a visit as soon as he touched down and after that, he would find his little bartender and make her pay for being disloyal.

Asaya walked into her condo and collapsed on the bed, exhausted from the day's activities and the humid air. She had started the day with group exercise and after eating breakfast, Lisa led the women on a hike of Manana Trail in Pearl City. The trail was four miles long and by the time they made it back down, everyone was starving. They picnicked right there at the park near the trailhead. This was more physical activity than Asaya had seen over the last four years. That, combined with the fresh and healthy diet the resort provided, made it impossible for her to hold on to the weight she had gained. The clothes she bought the day she left Seattle were hanging off her like drapes. Tomorrow was Sunday and that would be everyone's rest and relaxation day, so no retreat-related activities would take place. The break would give Asaya time to go to the local mall and get some clothes that fit her new body. She rolled over and pushed herself off the bed, before getting into the shower. The tepid water cascading over her dark chocolate skin was like heaven. If it were possible to sleep standing up, she would have done it. Asaya turned off the shower and lumbered back over to the bed. She picked up the phone and dialed Mrs. Johnson's number. She stayed on as long as she could, telling her mother about everything she had done since they last spoke and bragging about how much smaller she had gotten. After getting the latest news from the home front, Little J got on the phone to speak to his mommy. Hearing her baby sound happy and knowing he was in his granny's care put Asaya's mind at ease and after wishing them a good night, she laid back on the pillow and drifted into a deep sleep.

Bang, bang, bang!

Asaya sat straight up in the bed, trying to focus on where the loud noise was coming from.

Bang, bang, bang, bang!

She realized somebody was at the door. "Who is it?" she yelled. No one answered. She went to the door and looked out the peephole. Whoever it was, stood to the side so she could not see them. She could see the brim of his hat, but it was apparent that he did not want her to know who it was. Alarm set in and Asaya ran to the kitchen and grabbed a butcher knife off the counter. The mystery man was still knocking as she tiptoed back to the door and quietly unlocked it. She turned the knob and snatched the door open with one hand, while wielding her knife in the other.

"Oh shit! Put that down!" Rey exclaimed as he backed up a few steps. She threw the shank to the floor and jumped out the door, excited to see her closest friend. Rey was caught off guard when she wrapped her arms around his neck and kissed his cheek repeatedly. Saya was never this open and affectionate. It felt strange. Or maybe the way he involuntarily reacted to it was the strange part. It felt like he had received some kind of an electric shock. His body did things it had never done around her before. He quickly placed his hands on her waist and pushed her back a couple of feet.

"What's wrong?" she asked, innocently looking into his face in search of answers. Rey decided he was tripping and did not want to give her any cause for concern.

"Nothing's wrong, Saya. Just wanted to have a look at you... wow! You look great! What you been doing out here?" he inquired.

She unabashedly twirled around like she was walking the runway, grinning from ear-to-ear. "Everything! I want to tell you all about it. Come in!" she ordered, as she took his hand and pulled him into her suite. Before sitting down on the couch, he picked up the knife by the front door and returned it to the kitchen counter. They both laughed at the fact that she was ready to murder him.

Rey and Asaya stayed up until the sun came up. They talked about her adventures in Oahu, all the new things she had done, her new outlook on life; he was pleasantly surprised to see how much progress she had made. Physically, her body was so on point, it reminded him of the good old days when he had to beat the thirsty dudes off with a stick. She was obviously taking much better care of herself and her figure. But to him, the most amazing part of it all was her smile. It was what drew him to her as a kid and now it was back. It was nice to see her glowing and happy. It was important to him that he reiterated how much he supported her decision and had her back. She wanted to know about every little detail of his grocery store venture, and was excited over it like it was *her* dream. He stopped short of sharing what had happened at the club, because he did not want anything to put a damper on her mood. Easy conversation made the hours fly by and when the sun started to come up, they both agreed, they needed to go to bed. Asaya walked him to the door and hugged him tightly once again.

Again, Rey's body started to tingle from the interaction. He released her and walked off toward the elevator to return to his room.

KING JAMES

Waking up on Sunday morning really put the reality of the Buchanan's situation into perspective for James. Typically, he would make sure he was home on this day, because although his wife believed he did not care about her, he knew this was a sacred time for her and wanted to be part of her ritual. Asaya would get up, clean, and cook breakfast for the family. J now knew there was nothing like coming home after a week of non- stop running around to a neat house, a delicious home-cooked meal, and a beautiful lady that took good care of your mini-me. He would never have told her how much he appreciated her contribution, but now he was wondering if that was a mistake.

He rolled over and bumped right into Tanya on the other side of the bed. She was sound asleep with full make-up and weave on. James wondered to himself, *who does that?* Lately when he was missing his family, he would get upset and snap on her, but she was still here. It was not her fault he did not love her. He did this a lot; spent time with random chicks and made them feel special. But when they caught feelings and wanted him to leave his family, they had to go. Not once had he made such a bad decision as bringing one home to his castle. He had let Asaya's disappearance push him into making emotional moves and now Tanya had made herself at home in *his* house. James wanted her gone, but did not know how to undo the damage he had done.

He let Tanya leave her man to be with him because he needed a boost to his ego after his wife left him. Now it was going to damn near take an act of God to get her up out of here. The day he stayed at his mother-in-law's house, Tanya made it crystal clear that she was psycho and was not going to be pushed aside. At least his lady had moved beyond the "tearing up the house" phase. Starting that all over with someone else was a headache J did not need.

People had tried to convince him the he should not assume Asaya left, and he should be more concerned about her "disappearance". J was many things, but stupid was not one of them. He recalled how punk ass Officer Williams investigated and made it clear that he thought Mrs. Buchanan had left of her own free will, so the missing person's case was closed. When he came to let James know, he looked like the cat that ate the canary. On top of that, his mother-in-law suddenly stopped being distraught over her little girl. Nowadays she was all smiles and happy to keep her grandson all day every day. He knew how close Asaya was with her nosey ass mom and there was no way she

68

would be in a good mood if she was still in limbo about her daughter's status.

Now that James had time to think about his relationship with his lady, he could not be mad at her family for not wanting to be upfront with him. He knew Annette was the next best thing to a mommy for his son, so he allowed her to spend as much time with the little guy as she wanted. Besides, between the drug-induced stupor that lost his guy's club and his life savings, and the disintegration of his household, he was starting to believe his girl was right when she suggested he needed help. James sat up with his legs over the side of the bed. "Hey, baby. Good morning!" Tanya greeted with a smile on her face.

He returned the greeting so unenthusiastically, she barely heard him. She jumped out the bed and grabbed his robe for him, standing there and waiting until he stood so she could wrap it around him. It was a kind gesture, but all he could think about was how she looked exactly the same as she did at the club last night. He wondered if Tanya would wash yesterday's make-up off and replace it with a few fresh layers. James went over to the walk-in closet to grab a suit and tie before heading to the shower. He glanced over at Asaya's side only to find that all of her belongings were gone, replaced with skimpy clothes and stiletto heels in every color. He ran back into the room and grabbed Tanya by her arm.

"Where is my wife's shit?" he questioned angrily.

Scared by his aggression, Tanya stammered before replying, "It's-I-I moved it to the garage... I needed to put my stuff in here. She doesn't live—"

J shook her so hard Tanya thought he was going to snatch her arm out of socket. "Don't ever touch shit in this house without permission! Do you understand me?" His angry face was so close to hers, saliva misted her face with every word.

Unable to speak, she just nodded her head. When he finally let her go, she backed up and sat on the edge of the bed with tears threatening to run down her face. But Tanya was not crying because she was hurt. She was pissed off. *How dare he grab me like that over this bum ass broad?* she thought. She recalled the past week and how he had let her think she was the queen of this castle, but it turned out she was just a replacement. She concluded that she was nobody's wife; just a sidepiece who did not mean shit but a little recreational ass. He would not even bring his son home anymore while she was there; like he thought she was unfit to be around children or something. Tanya knew she had gotten too comfortable too fast. She needed to figure out what more she could do to make sure she was the best woman for J. She figured bonding with his rug rat and a cooking lesson couldn't hurt.

It seemed like James stayed in the shower forever. After giving him sufficient time to wash, Tanya slipped out of her nightie and entered the bathroom to try to make up for her misstep. As she slid the shower curtain back, she saw J standing there with his back to her. He had one arm raised against the shower wall and was resting his head on it. If she did not know any better, she would swear he was in here crying. The sound of the curtain sliding caught James attention. He put one hand out and in one stiff-arm motion, pushed Tanya out of the shower. He was not interested in any extracurricular activities right now. There was too much on his mind. Embarrassed by the rebuff, she grabbed a towel and exited in a flash. By the time he was out and fully dressed, Tanya had made a trip to the local IHOP and picked up a ham and cheese omelet for him. She ran up to him with the entrée as he was descending the spiral staircase. "Here, boo. I got you something to eat," she offered.

James' face twisted in a look of disgust. "You know I don't eat pork. What's—" he stopped speaking mid-sentence. He suddenly realized she did not know that because she did not know him. Mad at himself for moving a stranger in, he grabbed his keys off the table near the front door and left. In the driveway, he stopped to admire the new candy red paint job on his S Series. He had finally picked it up from the shop on Friday evening and it looked too clean to drive. That car was the type you would only see on a showroom floor. Instead of getting into his whip, he got into Asaya's gold Altima and drove off.

Mrs. Johnson was in the front yard trimming her bushes, while JJ played with his toys on a blanket nearby. He was dressed to the nines in some slacks and the tiniest little blue cardigan and button up shirt. His daddy had called this morning and asked her if she could get him ready for church by ten.

Annette was amused by the idea of her devil of a son-in-law actually stepping foot in the house of the Lord. Hell surely must have frozen over. James said he was going to Christ the King for service and you could have knocked Mrs. Johnson over with a feather. Asaya and Little J went there from time to time and she used to practically beg her husband to join them. He had usually just returned home from being gone for days, so he said he just wanted to chill on Sundays. Once, a couple of months back, she finally convinced him to come and worship with her. About fifteen minutes into the sermon, J had his head back on the pew with slobber running down his face and snoring like a buzz saw. Asaya elbowed him, trying inconspicuously to wake him up, but he went off and made a scene. He yelled at her about how she was trying to control him and cursed repeatedly, much to the chagrin of the congregation. He was asked to leave and she left with him due to humiliation. Since then, Asaya would not dare show her face there and did her best to avoid any of the church folk she ran into. When James stepped out of the car to get his son, Mrs. Johnson smiled warmly and complimented him. "You look nice!" she said.

"Thanks, Mom. I appreciate you getting him ready," he responded.

She wished them good luck at church and James could not help but giggle at her sarcasm. He strapped JJ into his car seat and chatted with him as he drove the short journey to Christ the King. In the short time with his grandma, Little J had added so many new words to his vocabulary, it seemed like he had been gone for years. *That lady definitely had a way with kids,* he thought.

James arrived at the church a few minutes late and could see that the sermon had already begun. He opened the door slowly and tried to slip in undetected, but the creaky old door made so much noise everyone turned around to see who could not make it to the house of God on time. Nervous because of all of the judgmental eyes on him, J hurried to the nearest empty seat where he sat with his son on his lap. He hoped no one would recognize him from the only other time he had been in the building. All of the ladies in the church made it obvious that was not the case. They took turns looking at him and whispering to one another. If he caught them staring, they would shake their heads to let him know they did not approve of his previous actions. The men did not want to be associated with J. He tried to make eye contact with the guys in the congregation, wanting to know that someone forgave and supported him, but they all gave him the cold shoulder. He thought about leaving, but was sure that would just draw even more attention to the "pariah" in the back of the room. He decided to wait it out, and eventually Pastor Smith called his parishioners' attention back to the scripture.

Today, Pastor read a scripture from Hebrews 13:5. "Keep your lives free from the love of money and be content with what you have, because God has said, 'Never will I leave you; never will I forsake you'." For some reason, it was like that passage was written specifically for James. He was obsessed with the love of money to the extreme that it

74

had torn apart his life and his family. Financial gain had been his priority, but not the only one. He could also directly relate to Timothy 3:2: Therefore, an overseer must be above reproach, the husband of one wife, sober-minded, self-controlled, respectable, hospitable and able to teach. J had been none of these things. He never really thought through the prospect of marriage and only did it so Asaya would not leave him after catching him doing dirt for the umpteenth time. He said all of the words you are expected to say when you are getting married, but thought of it more as part of the ceremony than words to live by. She took it literally and expected the same from him.

The pressure was too much and after a while, James just said *fuck it* and did what he felt like doing. For J, it was much easier to disregard Asaya's feelings, than to try to live life by her rules. There was no question in his mind that the other qualities like sober-minded, self-controlled and hospitable did not apply to him. It was evident by all of the events that were taking place in his life. He looked down at his son, who was smiling and clapping on his lap as the choir sang, "Victory". He could see why Asaya was in such good spirits after attending church and was sorry he had ruined that for her and JJ. He felt tears welling up in his eyes and for the first time in his adult life, he let them fall freely.

Little J looked up and used the sleeve of his shirt to wipe his daddy's face.

After service ended, Pastor Smith walked up to J and introduced himself. The two men talked for a few minutes before James was asked to join the pastor in the back office. He, too, had recognized James from their previous encounter and wanted to see if there was anything he could do to help the young man. When they were out of earshot of the rest of the patrons, Pastor Smith asked questions about Asaya and her whereabouts. He did not ask why she had not attended in a while because the answer to that question was obvious to him. After hearing the details of what had occurred over the last week, he prayed over James and Little J and for Asaya. It was good to be in the company of another man that understood his mistakes, forgave them and was ready to show him how to move forward. J promised to come back next week. He left Christ the King feeling a certain clarity. He had always known he was doing a lot of things that had a negative effect in his life and the lives of people around him. J was good at ignoring remorse or drowning it in drugs and alcohol. He now knew it was time to face his problems head on and start dealing with them like a man.

It was late in the evening when James finally pulled back

up in front of the Johnson home. Annette came running outside. "Where have y'all been?" she inquired. "I was worried sick. I tried calling you, but it was going to voicemail."

He explained to her that after church he wanted to spend some uninterrupted time with his son, so he powered off the phone and took JJ out to eat and to the park. The little boy was knocked out in the back seat, so J carried him into the house for Mrs. Johnson. After making sure he was tucked in and comfortable, he jumped back on the road to head home.

James pulled into the driveway of his home. It used to feel like a refuge from everything out there in the world, but now he was hesitant to go in and face this woman he barely knew. He regretted dragging her into the mess he created. He would need to do whatever it took to get her out. When J walked into the door, he was surprised by the smell of food cooking. He walked into the kitchen to find Tanya with an apron draped over her little red dress and recipes she had printed scattered all over the kitchen counter. He lifted the lid on a pot on the stove and looked inside to find collard greens simmering. They smelled delicious, but he had learned that when it came to Tanya's cooking, aromas could be deceiving. On further inspection, he also found a pot roast and homemade cornbread in the dual ovens, mashed potatoes, candied yams and a sweet potato pie. J figured that this layout must have taken her all day to put together, especially with her homemaking skills. She looked up from the list of ingredients she was studying and smiled at him. She rushed over to him, threw her arms around his neck and kissed his cheek softly. He pulled away slightly, but not enough for her to notice. "Hey, baby, did you have a good day?" she cooed.

"It was cool. How about you?" he countered, feigning concern. She went about telling him about all the housework she had done while he was away, and giving him the play by play on how much effort she put into the soul food she had prepared. He could see she was trying to impress him and considered his next move for a moment before deciding the bad news could wait.

James went upstairs and changed into a t-shirt and a pair of basketball shorts to lounge around the house in. When he returned, he saw that the dining room table had been set. Asaya's decorative scented candles had been lit to set the mood. It took every bit of self-control in him not to flash about Tanya crossing boundaries like he did in the closet this morning. He closed his eyes, took a deep breath and let his ire dissipate. J repeatedly told himself it was just candles. He would be sure to make a trip to Bed, Bath & Beyond and replace them tomorrow. He tasted the dinner Tanya had prepared and it was not bad. Of course, it was not the kind of cooking he had grown accustomed to, but it was a good try. James wanted to eat his meal in silence but Tanya made it impossible with her back-to-back questions about his background. She was attempting to get to know him because she was self-conscious about the IHOP incident this morning. In an attempt not to be rude, J gave her short answers to her inquiries. After many tries, she gave up and finished her meal quietly. He finished eating and plopped down on the new sofa to watch *SportsCenter*. He could hear Tanya in the kitchen banging around pots and pans while she straightened up, to let him know she was completing yet another task on his behalf. He turned the volume up on the television to drown out the background noise.

Tanya soon joined J after her work was done. She tried to get his attention by kissing on his neck, but he leaned his head toward her to limit access. So Tanya did the only thing that was sure to work every time. She dropped to her knees in front of J and began unbuckling his pants. Not one to turn down some easy oral satisfaction, James relaxed and closed his eyes. Try as he might, he just could not get his manhood to respond to all of the attention it was receiving; it just lay on his right thigh like a damp washcloth. Sensing that her seduction techniques were not achieving the desired outcome, Tanya stood up and began to undress for him. She was aware of how much he loved her body and knew there was no way he could resist. She made the job of getting naked more time consuming and difficult than it should have been, hoping to entice her prey with perfect curves and 'accidental' gyrations. Every time she wiggled slowly and purposely in one direction, J would move to the opposite direction, not wanting to miss the highlights from the NBA games. Exasperated with the corny cat and mouse game Tanya was playing, James took her by the wrists aggressively to still her movements. She had a bewildered expression on her face that let him know she was puzzled as to what was going on. As she stood there in nothing more than a Victoria's Secret thong, J forcefully sat her down on the couch near him. She stared in his face bracing for what was to come. "Okay, listen…" he started, "I know I brought you in here during a rough time and gave you a lot of expectations. You really are cool people and my intention was never to fuck you over." She sat in silence, knowing what was coming, but hoping she was wrong. James continued with what he was saying, determined to get this

80

off his chest and over with. "I'm not trying to hop right into a new relationship like this... I mean, I don't even know what's going to happen with my marriage situation...we don't really know each other. I'm sorry, but you have to move out... I know you lost your spot messing with me, so I will pay for you to move in somewhere and give you a few months' rent to help, but I need you to be gone by the end of the week."

Tanya just sat there, too stunned to speak. She did her best not to show how pissed off she was. Unsure what to do or say, she grabbed her clothing off the floor and ran upstairs to the bedroom, slamming the door behind her. James felt like a load of bricks had been lifted off his shoulders. He fell to sleep in front of the television to the sounds of Charles Barkley and Kenny "The Jet" Smith commentating on today's games.

CLOSER

Rey dropped Asaya's shopping bags on the couch in her vacation rental. After interrupting her sleep last night, he had waited until almost noon to call her today. When he finally did, they agreed to get out and have lunch, and see what Oahu had to offer a tourist. They decided to go to Honolulu and walked around to different eateries, sampling things like mahi-mahi, malasadas and shaved ice. They shared a pupu platter and Rey kept going, eating a loco moco. Asaya watched him as he grubbed, thinking there was no way she was eating that after all of the hard work she had put in over the past week. Over lunch, they talked about the old days at the Lakeside School and all of the memories they shared. Asaya surprised Rey by telling him she had started writing again. In high school, she had won multiple scholarships for her writing and had been dubbed 'The Essay Queen'. She would write short stories and publish them in the *Lakeside Legend*, plays for the drama club, and create posts for the school's intranet. At the UW, she was able to complete her Bachelor of Science degree in journalism early and planned to be a bestselling author or a news writer. Rey personally thought she could be a news reporter; she had the looks for it.

After college, Asaya had met James Buchanan and all of her aspirations fell by the wayside. J thought all that writing was a waste of time and preferred she take care of the house in her spare time. Without the encouragement from Rey and her peers, Saya started to believe it was not worth the time investment she was making. But she truly loved writing and as part of her reinvention during this retreat, decided to start slow by composing one page essays on different subjects. When she picked up the pen and pad, the story of her life just poured out onto the pages and before you knew it, she was halfway through the making of a full novel. Asaya pulled out her notepad and Rey was astonished at how much writing she had done in such a short time. She would not let him read it yet, but by the elated smile on her face and the way her eyes lit up when she spoke about it, he knew it would be a good read. It was so good to have the girl he knew and loved back, but it was different this time. He could not quite place his finger on what had changed between them, but was convinced it was for the better. Rey let her know he was down to do whatever it took to help her reach her goals.

They went to the Ala Moana Center, a large open air shopping mall, and visited Nordstrom and Macy's, along with several more of the almost three hundred retailers available. The place was packed with other visitors, along with many of the locals, but the environment was laid back. Everywhere they entered, customers and staff members either complimented him on what a beautiful wife he had or told them that they were a stunning couple. It was an easy assumption to make, them being in a vacation spot and the glimmering wedding ring on Asaya's hand that sparkled in the sunlight with every gesture. He had to admit, they did look good together. Ultimately, they got tired of straightening people out on their status and started saying thank you and moving on. She seemed to be unfazed by the assumption that they were a couple, but Rey felt a sense of pride as they strolled through the mall together. *This is stupid,* he thought, *I'm feeling myself like this is my woman.* He shook his head and stepped away from Asaya as if that would bring him back to his senses. She looked over at him and asked, "What's wrong with you?"

"Nothing..." he replied and pretended he moved away to look at something in a storefront window. She brushed off his strange behavior and continued exploring. Rey went into a sportswear store to shop while Asaya made a beeline to Nordstrom to pick up a few pairs of new high heels. All the shoes in her closet were tennis shoes, flats, wedges, or super low heels. She had not bought a fierce pair of shoes in years because there was really nowhere to wear them. While her home girls went clubbing on the weekend, she spent her time at the house with Little J. They would always have juicy stories about who James was with at the club, or him trying to get in the pants of one of her close friends, so she stayed away from the nightlife to avoid drama. But things had changed so much Asaya was ready to get her youth and her life back. She would not necessarily start frequenting nightclubs, but she was definitely going to be stepping out and getting grown and sexy on a regular.

Rey opened the door to the waiting Town Car and waited for Asaya to slide in. She was wearing a short zebra print skirt, so she sat down first, then pulled her legs into the car, masterfully keeping them tightly together to avoid a free peepshow to the passersby. Her legs were the longest, smoothest legs Rey had ever seen. The baby oil she had hydrated them with made them look like milk chocolate melting in the sun. Unintentionally, his mind wandered to thoughts of reaching down and running his hand up and down the length of her thighs, or better yet, planting soft kisses all over them.

"Are you going to shut the door?" Asaya joked. Jolted from his daydream, Rey slammed the door and put the shopping bags into the trunk. "Are you okay, Rey?" she quizzed, looking more distressed than earlier. "Ever since the mall, you seem to be somewhere else. Did I say something to offend you?"

He smiled, grabbed her hand and reassured her that everything was good. "Nah, Saya. I just had a little business on my mind. You know me… it's hard to keep my mind off my hustle. We cool."

Satisfied with his explanation, Asaya sat back and relaxed. They rode back toward the resort, quietly reflecting on the day's events. The day had been wonderful and she did not want it to end.

"You know what I want to do?" Not waiting for a response, she answered, "I want to go out and dance. I haven't been out dancing in forever!"

Rey was tired physically, but never too drained to put a smile on his friend's face. "Okay. I'm with it. Where you wanna go?" he asked.

"I heard of this place called the Underground. They're supposed to have good music and good service." It was refreshing to ask for something and actually get it! Asaya loved dancing, but every time she invited her husband to join her, he was not in the mood to dance, yet she would hear about how he was freaking the next chick all night at the club. After so many rejections she had settled on the fact that dancing was a thing of the past. Today was a new beginning and she was excited.

When they arrived back at the Hawaiian Princess Resort, Rey carried Asaya's bags to her room for her and once again, entered the elevator to return to his own suite. They would both get showered and dressed, and she would come up to his room to get him when she was done; that way she did not feel rushed. Asaya stepped in front of the mirror after throwing on her tropical print dress and the matching heels she had picked up today. Her body was almost unrecognizable. Her waist had shrunk tremendously and everything looked perfect. Her new body made the outfit seem too provocative. Waving off the tinge of insecurity, Asaya applied lipstick and eyeliner. After exiting her room, she took the elevator to the top floor of the resort. When she exited, there were only three doors on the whole floor. She gently knocked at room 1501. Rey opened the door and looked her up and down. In all the years he had known Asaya, she had never dressed this sexy. He knew she had a nice body, but this dress showed exactly how hard she had worked on her figure. He attempted to greet her casually, but his stomach was in knots at the sight of her. Rey was not the only one feeling butterflies about the platonic outing. Asaya surveyed the prime piece of real estate standing before her. He had on some designer jeans that hung low on his hips so you could see the imprint of his entire six-pack through the white wife beater he was wearing. Rey usually wore tank tops in the summertime, but in the past, Asaya made sure she diverted her attention to avoid any impure thoughts about her childhood friend. But here, in this environment, she was able to take it all in without feeling like she had broken the law. She moved her eyes slowly from his chest to his arms and shoulders. "Damn", she mumbled to herself, forcing her eyes to move to his face before she started to drool. He flashed a smile that exposed all of his perfect white teeth... and those lips.

"Hello? You coming in or you just gone stand there looking at me like I'm crazy?" Rey interjected. Asaya brushed past him, ashamed of her obvious attraction. She looked around the room and her jaw damn near dropped to the floor. She had no idea Rey was up in here living like a king. This must have been the penthouse suite. The floors were made of marble and the living room area was filled with the most contemporary furnishings and artwork. Everything was red, black and white. Far off in the corner of the living room, was a hot tub. Asaya wondered who in the hell needed a hot tub in the living room.

A huge projector screen acted as a wall between the

living room and the kitchen. She could see through the double doors that led to the master suite and the bed looked as big as a swimming pool. There were barely any walls in the suite, just windows that provided an awesome view of the resort's surroundings. "Damn, boy! You didn't tell me you were up here living like this!" she exclaimed. Rey just laughed because they both knew that no matter what it was, he liked to do it big. She glanced at the coffee table in the living room and saw that he had a collection of all of the newest movies at the box office. She did not even ask how he got his hands on them. She picked up an oldie, but goodie. "*Love & Basketball*! I haven't seen this in years!" Asaya reminisced.

"Let's watch it after we get back," Rey replied.

"Okay, cool. Now let's go." They went to the lobby where their driver was patiently waiting.

When they pulled up to the Underground, the line was wrapped around the building. Asaya sighed, dreading the long wait to get in. They exited the vehicle and walked past the waiting patrons to the front of the line. Rey exchanged words with the doorman, and then took her hand, leading her into the spot. Asaya laughed to herself; *of course, he has a hook up here, too*! They walked directly over to the VIP lounge and were immediately greeted by a cute little waitress, wearing a pair of barely-there Daisy Duke's and crop top. She made her interest in Rey evident, despite the presence of his obvious companion. Asaya was used to chicks outright hitting on James. She was also used to him flirting back. It happened so much that instead of getting uncomfortable, she would simply walk away. For some reason, her heart started beating fast at this blatant disrespect from the waitress. She looked around the club nervously in an attempt to diffuse the aggravation. To her surprise, Rey offered no response to the woman's advances. She was pretty enough and he was single; Asaya wondered what the issue was. Once the hostess walked away, she grilled him about his love life. "Why did you turn her down? She was cute. Are you with someone? How come you never bring her around?"

Rey chuckled at her questions before answering, "Yes, she was cute... No, I'm not in a relationship. I'm just focused on my goals right now. I figure I got time... and I haven't really come across anyone I was feeling like that, you know."

Asaya sarcastically replied, "I don't know how much time you got... You already in your early thirties. You better start looking. I know you at least have a homie-lover-friend to see just to... you know what I mean."

Rey paused, unsure if he should share this much personal information, then responded, "I actually don't. I did up until

about three months ago. She wanted more and I was not into her like that. I been working on practicing self-discipline. I don't want to keep using broads…I mean women for sex." Asaya looked at him waiting for an indication that he was kidding, but he was serious. The intense conversation was interrupted when the waitress returned with the drinks. They were both lightweights, so the first round had them buzzing. As they were sipping on round two, a handsome local guy politely asked her for a dance and she accepted. He was nowhere near as fine as Rey, but she thought if she danced with him, her friend would feel more comfortable socializing with some of the females that were ogling him since they arrived. She wanted him to have a good time and did not want to become his ball and chain on her vacation. Caught off guard by Asaya's interaction with her new suitor, Rey did not hesitate when one of the island girls took his hand and pulled him to the dance floor. She started dancing sensually to Beyoncé's "Baby Boy" and rubbing up against him as he did his two-step. As sexy as his partner was, he could not help looking across the dance floor to see if

Asaya was enjoying herself. He knew immediately she had drunk one too many cocktails. She was seductively rotating her hips to the beat of the music and her slinky dress had ridden midway up her voluptuous thighs. The dude she was dancing with was barely moving back and forth, entranced by her suggestive gyrations. He kept running his hands up and down her waist, going further south with each touch and licking his lips in anticipation. Rey's first instinct was to knock him out, but he did not want to humiliate Asaya when she was having so much fun. However, if dude's hand went below the waist, he would have to draw the line. Island Girl followed Rey's eyes to find out whom or what was taking his attention off of her. She saw that it was the same woman he had come with, and decided to step her game up. She turned away from him and backed her butt up against his shaft, surprised that it was not standing at attention after all the work she had put in. When the song switched to Wale's "Bad", Island Girl made sure she used her sexiest moves to entice the suave stranger. Rey was still keeping his eyes on the guy that had his hands all over Asaya. Finally, he got up the nerve to move his hands down and palm her booty. She stopped dancing and drew back her hand to slap the shit out of him. Before she could react, Rey had moved Island Girl to the side and got in between Asaya and her dance partner. The man knew he was not equipped to fight, so he backed off and exited. Rey tried to take Asaya's arm and pull her back to the seating area, but she wanted to keep dancing.

"Wait… no! I'm good, Rey. I still want to dance…" she demanded. Knowing he could not convince her otherwise, he conceded. He stayed on the floor and danced with her, because he did not want anyone else misreading her tipsy antics. She wrapped her arms around his neck and their bodies were pressed together like two magnets. His mind told him the best thing to do would be to pull away, but his body was doing its own thing. He wrapped his arms around her waist as she continued the circular hip motions he had previously watched from afar.

Rey was not much of a dancer, but he found himself mirroring her movements like they choreographed this performance. He could feel his erection growing, but this time he did not make an effort to hide it. He reasoned with himself that nothing was wrong with letting his best friend know she was alluring. He could feel Asaya's peppermint breath against the side of his neck and could smell the fruity scent of her lotion. His lips inadvertently brushed against her ear and it made his mouth water. He wanted to run his tongue over her ear and down her neck, but gained his composure before turning his thoughts into action.

Asaya could not be sure whether it was Rey, making her feel like this or the drinks. His body felt warm against hers and his arms around her waist seemed to be on fire. At one point, his lips swept over her ear and made her tingle all over. For a brief moment, she fantasized about those lips roaming all over her body. Asaya swore she felt Rey's manhood pressing into her lower abdomen, but did not want to make assumptions. But if that was what he was working with, it was no wonder women did any and everything to be in his company.

As the song came to an end, she released his neck and he loosened his grip on her. She looked up at him, hoping she had not made things between them too awkward. He was peering down at her and his eyes were low. If Asaya did not know any better, she would say Rey wanted to fuck the shit out of her right there on the dance floor. The thought automatically made her lick her lips. "Oh my goodness," she said, shaking her head. "I'm sorry, Rey. I was drunk and—"

He cut her off. "It's okay, Saya. We both had too much to drink. Let's get outta here." He held her hand and guided her to the car. On the ride home, it seemed as if the lusty moment at the Underground never happened. They talked about how much they enjoyed the spot and even joked about their thirsty dance partners.

By the time Rey and Asaya returned to the Hawaiian Princess Resort, their light buzz had worn off and they were back to being best friends. "It's early. We're squares! You wanna watch movies still?" Rey asked, making sure Asaya did not feel uncomfortable. "Of course! Can I use your Jacuzzi?" she responded.

"Hell yeah! I was going to get in there anyway... sip some lightweight bubbly... take advantage of my investment."

They stopped by Asaya's room so she could grab a bathing suit and some loungewear to put on afterward. She showered and changed into her swimsuit in Rey's bathroom and stood there for a minute, afraid to walk out in front of him. This was the first time in her life she had worn a bathing suit, and this was actually a bikini. Even when she had no weight issues, she was never one to show off her figure. Asaya finally worked up the nerve and walked out the bathroom, pretending to be confident. Rey was in the middle of setting up *Love & Basketball* on the projector.

Asaya's plan was to make a beeline for the hot tub and hide her body in the water, but he had not gotten around to filling it yet, so she was forced to stand there exposed. "Do you want me to run the water?" she offered.

He looked up from what he was doing, but did not say anything. Rey had already had to keep his libido in line at the Underground when Saya was in a skimpy outfit. Now she was almost naked in a red string bikini. He finally responded to her.

"Yes, please. I'm gonna go take a shower. Can you bring over the wine and glasses, too? And the snack tray I made us?"

Eager to move away from the visual examination he was conducting, she replied, "Yeah, sure."

While Rey showered, Asaya prepared everything so they could start the movie as soon as he finished. The water had run and she hopped in up to her chest and poured herself a glass of Moscato to stop the butterflies from fluttering around in her stomach. It made no sense to be this jittery, she assured herself. *It's just Rey!* She downed the first glass and poured a second, eager to get past any uneasy feelings before he returned.

Rey dipped his head under the streaming water in the shower. He was trying his best to convince himself that he was not attracted to Asaya. That she was only a friend; that she was off limits because she was his best friend's wife.

When he felt his willpower was strong enough, he got out, dried off and slipped on his fitted boxers. He strolled out of the bathroom, stopped to grab the remote control and walked over to the hot tub. Asaya had obviously had a couple of drinks because she looked him over head to toe, as if he were a cold drink of water on a hot day in the desert. She could not believe how magnificent his body was. She could see why his little booty call had been trying to lock him down. Rey hit play on the movie as he sank down into the tub. Asaya grabbed his glass and poured him some Moscato, and handed it to him dutifully; she would not be the only one that was tipsy in this bitch. He gulped it down in record time and turned to watch the show. For the first ten minutes, Rey did his best to stay focused on the movie and not on the chocolate beauty in red just feet away from him. The mission failed when Saya jumped up and needed to rush to the bathroom because of all the wine she had drunk. Initially, he could feel that she was not comfortable in her own skin, but two glasses of wine later, she walked across the room like she owned it, flaunting her thick, juicy cakes every step of the way. Rey watched every sway of her hips until she disappeared from sight. The water dripping off her body made her even more enticing, if that was possible.

Once again, he worked on calming his erection while she was gone. She returned, looking a lot more composed than before and climbed back in. After drying her hands, she nibbled on the fresh fruit, cheese, and crackers Rey had prepared. Still feeling flirtatious, Asaya looked at Rey provocatively and asked, "Do you want some?"

He responded carefully, unsure of what exactly she was offering. "Some food?"

"Yes, some food," she giggled. He moved toward the tray on Asaya's side of the hot tub to pick something to eat from the snack tray. First, he ate a couple of fresh strawberries and then opted for a slice of pineapple. She watched his mouth while he ate, debating whether or not she wanted to sample a piece of the fruit from his mouth.

Asaya knew she should not be coming onto her best friend, but truth be told, she always loved him… and not just in a platonic way. She fell in love with him the first day they met in fifth grade at Lakeside. He was a little rough around the edges, but a really sweet and gentle guy. Initially, she dreamed of them growing up and getting married, having kids and living happily ever after. But as they grew closer, she did not want to ruin the best friendship she would ever have, so she buried her feelings deep inside and kept them hidden.

At times, it was hard to refrain from just jumping his bones; especially the nights when she was hurt or lonely and he listened to her, comforted her and held her for hours on end. So much had changed now. They were thousands of miles from home and James. Besides, she had not been affectionately touched by a man in months. Her man was too busy giving his time to every other random chick he could. Even when he did stumble in high or drunk trying to get some, Asaya was too disgusted to do it.

Yep, she decided that was it; she was going to live in the moment and enjoy herself tonight. There would be repercussions and she would deal with them another day. She got up and floated over to Rey. Uncertain as to what her intentions were, he slowly continued to eat the piece of pineapple in his mouth. She drifted into a straddle position on his lap and leaned down to remove a sample of pineapple from his mouth with hers.

Paralyzed by the unexpected actions, Rey sat there with his lips passionately parted, while Asaya searched his mouth with her tongue. After she retrieved the fruit, she sat straight up, waiting for his reaction. This was his chance to stop the madness; all he needed to do was reject her and she would back off. But there was no way he would push her away; Rey had been waiting for this moment for what

99

seemed like an eternity. When his parents decided to send him to Lakeside, he begged to go to school in the hood. There were hardly any kids like him at Lakeside and he wanted to be in familiar surroundings. The very first day of class, he met Saya; a pretty little dark-skinned girl, with shoulder-length wavy hair. He had never seen a girl that looked like her and thought she looked like his little sister's baby doll.

She was quiet and shy and did not talk much to anyone, but Rey made it a priority to befriend the girl. They became the best of friends and he never tried anything, because he did not want to do anything to hurt her. He wanted to wait until he was mature enough to be a good man to her, but J got to her before he could make his move. At first, he was pissed off at his boy for moving in on his territory, but when it became evident that things were serious between him and Saya, Rey backed off and charged it to the game. He had even confronted J before about being a snake because he was the only person that Rey told how he truly felt about Saya. J's only response was, "Hey, you snooze, you lose."

Rey was tempted to whoop his ass, but instead vowed to keep his private thoughts to himself from here on out. But none of that mattered right now. No one was here to get in the way. Now he was a grown ass man and she was a grown ass… sexy ass woman. Unable to hold back any longer, he placed his hands on her hips and ran them slowly up and down her thighs. He did not even make an effort to hide his fully engorged wood this time. He wanted her to know she turned him on. Asaya arched her back, closed her eyes and let out a soft moan when she felt his hardness between her legs. Rey put his hand on the small of her back and pulled her toward him. Her face was inches from his; he looked into her eyes to be sure that what was occurring was still okay. Even at this stage, if she changed her mind, he would stop and nurse a cold case of blue balls. But looking at each other only turned the temperature up on this forbidden love affair. The desire in her eyes made his whole body long to be against and inside of her. He pulled her closer and lightly brushed his lips against hers. That gesture alone almost brought Asaya to an orgasm. Rey traced the outline of her mouth with his tongue and she did her best not to pant like a dog in heat. She met his tongue with hers and the kiss went from delicate to hungry. She wrapped her legs around his waist to pull herself as close as possible, and he kept his hands on her hips to keep her there. She had never been kissed like this before. It was as if he was making love to her mouth; his tongue was moving seamlessly in and out of her mouth. His soft, succulent lips were sucking her tongue in and out of his mouth. His mouth trailed down her neck and he inhaled deeply, relishing her fragrance. He traveled back and forth from her neck to her ears, devouring her as if he were starving; he was sure to leave her first hickies where he had been. Her eyes opened when he leaned back and rested his head on the rim of the tub. Asaya sat straight up, wondering what was wrong. Rey was not looking at her, though. His eyes followed his hands as they trailed all over her body. She had never gotten the privilege of seeing his sex face and now understood why females practically threw the coochie at him left and right. But he was the type of man that was not out there slinging penis to every lady that wanted some. *Damn! What the fuck am I doing?* Asaya thought. Rey was a good guy; he was the type of man that would make some lady very lucky and happy someday. He was loyal, loving, fine as hell; everything her husband was not. She could not drag him into her mess. It was not fair to coerce him to waste his affections on a woman he could not be with. *For heaven's sake, I am married to his friend!* Asaya placed both hands on Rey's chest and pushed away. He sat up as she climbed off him and out of the tub. "You okay, Saya? What's wrong?" he asked.

"I-I'm sorry, Rey. I fucked up. I'm so sorry for doing this..." she pleaded.

"Wait, don't be sorry. We both did it. I'm not sorry…" he responded.

"J is your friend and I am married. I'm not like this." She grabbed her loungewear and her keys off

the table and ran out the door. He tried to throw on his bathrobe and run after her, but the elevator had closed before he could get there. Rey leaned back against the wall with his head in his hands for a minute before walking back into the penthouse.

THE TABLES TURN

Monday morning was a new start for James Buchanan. It had been a week since his wife left him and he had finally gotten around to giving Tanya a deadline to move out. He did not mind paying for her to get a spot because he knew it was the right thing to do. It seemed that all of the bad luck he had recently was more like karma coming back to bite him in the ass. He walked up the stairs and opened his room door. Tanya was lying in the bed fast asleep, but woke up when she heard him enter the bathroom. "Good morning," she greeted cheerfully.

J stuck his head back out the bathroom door, skeptical about the good mood she was in. "Good morning," he replied. She had a wide grin on her face and of course, was fully made up. He would not miss that make-up covered pillowcase at all when she was gone. After showering and getting dressed, J opened the safe in the back of his closet and took out a stack of money. He walked up to the foot of the bed and extended his hand to give it to Tanya.

She eagerly grabbed the money and counted it. "Twenty thousand dollars? How am I going to get a car?" she complained.

"I been living with you for a week, Tanya. Don't try to

play me. That's more than generous. Now get up, get dressed and find somewhere to stay!" James ordered.

She did not argue back, but obediently put on her clothes and called a cab to pick her up.

She still had a house key, for now, but opted to wait outside on the curb until her ride arrived. When James left, he sped right past her in the gold Altima without saying a word. He had made it clear that they were not a couple; therefore, they would not be painting the town red together. He did not even seem to want to be seen with her.

She had texted him yesterday about going to church with him and Little J, but got no response. "I guess I'm not good enough to take to service," she had said at the time. The more she sat there alone, the closer she came to the conclusion that he wanted nothing to do with her. She knew she was nothing more than a booty call to him. She searched the house, looking for clues as to what his raggedy ass Plain Jane of a wife did to keep him coming back. *She is cute enough, but ain't got nothin' on me. If she was not so fuckin' dull, she might even be a dime,* Tanya thought. But she kept the house clean, took good care of the little boy and obviously could throw down in the kitchen. If she was going to compete and trap his ass, Tanya knew she would have to learn to cook and have a bomb ass Sunday dinner prepared for J when he finally got back. She would have even given his spoiled brat something to eat, but he was sure to drop him off at his grandma's house before showing up. She recalled how she worked in that kitchen like a damn slave, and he still had the audacity to sit her down and tell her she had to kick rocks. This was the first time someone had made her feel this low and Tanya did what she did best. J gave her a little piece of his stack to get the fuck out of his face, so she would do just that, as soon as she found her next victim. But one thing was for damn sure; he would not get away with doing her dirty. She had navigated her way through the minnows to get her hands on a shark, only to be tossed aside like trash; someone would have to pay for this. She had a few moves of her own, so she called her business partner for assistance. He told her that he was out of town taking care of some family affairs and she could crash at one of his low-key spots while he was gone. It seemed like a nice move, but Tanya knew this was about nothing but work and for every favor he did her, she would be in debt to him. She and her partner had never been romantically involved, and not because she was not with it. Unlike most men she came across, he was not at all interested in bedding her. He could see she was a hustler and had a way with the fellows, so he added her to his team. He paid well and his only three requirements were that she followed instructions to the tee, she kept no secrets and she could never tell a soul that she even knew him. He had put her up to some grimy jobs and if she were to ever be connected to him, it would be World War III.

James drove past his soon-to-be ex-concubine sitting on the curb. He realized it was rude to keep driving past her, but wanted to make sure he was not giving mixed messages. She desperately wanted to be the next Mrs. Buchanan and that just was not in the cards. His goal was to be as stern as possible, but still be fair. The only thing she had done wrong was dealing with a married man and that was more on him than her. Right now, he just wanted to change the course of things and he needed to be upfront and honest with everybody. Usually he was uneasy about visiting Mrs. Johnson, because she was critical of everything he did. Lately he had been forced to spend more time around her, because he did not dare bring his son around Tanya.

He had come to realize that she was not all that bad, just an overprotective mother that did not want anyone hurting her daughter. James could definitely feel her on that because he felt just as strongly about his son. She was harsh, strict, judgmental and sometimes outright mean, but she was also all the things his mother never was: loving, caring, responsible, logical and just a good mom and grandmother. He had gained a new appreciation for her knack of getting all in everyone's business. She was able to give him good advice and direct him when he was lost. "Hey, son," she greeted when he walked in, "I got the baby dressed and ready for you."

James sat down on the couch, unsure of where to start. "I actually needed to talk with you, Mom."

Annette stopped packing the bag and looked at him. "Okay. Go ahead," she invited. J confessed everything to his mother-in-law; not leaving a detail out. He figured she would hate him for it, but it was important to get it off his chest. They talked about all of the cheating he had done, miscellaneous women Asaya had confronted and fought because of his infidelity; he even told her about Tanya and shared the fact that she was staying in the house.

He waited for Mrs. Johnson to jump up and go crazy on him, but she sat there calmly listening.

When he finished, she told him a story of her own. She talked about how Mr. Johnson had put her through many of the same things in their younger days and that one day he had come to his senses and changed his ways. James was surprised to find out that such a perfect couple had experienced the same issues he and his wife had. She also let him know that she knew about all of it before he even told her. Although her daughter had stopped sharing their problems, she had eyes and ears everywhere. Annette made it clear that she did not want her grandbaby being mothered by someone else and J agreed. In return for his compliance, he asked that she be upfront with him as well. He wanted her to tell him where his girl was, but would settle for the peace of mind of hearing she was safe and secure. Mrs. Johnson felt bad for leading James to believe Asaya had simply disappeared and thought it was only right to ease his stress. "I can tell you that I have talked to her and she is okay. A person can only take so much before they break down, son. I respect you for coming clean and it looks like you are ready to change, but you gotta let her have time to deal with what she went through."

He nodded in agreement and grabbed Little J and left. Now that he knew his wife was alright, he could focus on putting their lives back together.

Little J was in a much better mood after spending time with his grandmother. He sang happily as they pulled up to the childcare center. He had not been here in a few days and James hoped he would not cry when his daddy left him. Truth be told, J preferred that his boy ride with him all day, but right now it was imperative that he make sure he tie up any loose ends on the hustle tip, check in on his medical marijuana venture to be sure it is working as efficiently as possible, and start this Silver Spoon renovation project.

He hated to admit it, but Will was on point when he said that J was spending too much time playing and not enough working. He definitely needed to refocus his energy, so if it was not about his family or his endeavors, it had to go. He was relieved when JJ ran into his classroom, hugged his teacher, and then cheerfully began playing with his friends. He must have missed his routine; J made a note-to-self that no matter what was going on, from now on he would try to maintain a sense of normalcy for his boy.

James traveled about forty-five-minutes northeast of Seattle, to the city of Woodinville. He had chosen this area to set up his commercial gardening operation because it was out of the way, and there was no chance of running into someone that recognized him. The only person that was privy to his lucrative enterprise was Asaya, and her allegiance to him made her as discreet about it as he was. He had not even told Will or Rey that he had taken his game to the next level. He trusted them but felt it was okay for a man to have something that was only his on the side. There was a crew of five laborers that James had hired and these guys were not from the town. He made sure he selected white boys that had already been growing and smoking for years. They needed to know exactly what they were doing and what strains were first-rate. They even had testing equipment in the building and carried top-of-the-line weed like Jack Kevorkian, Wonder Woman, Sour Diesel and every superb plant of the Kush variety you could think of. Demand was high and earnings were through the roof. He ran extensive background checks on all of them, swore them to a confidentiality agreement, and still took additional steps to protect his profits. He had hired a private investigator to find out where each of his employees laid their head and who they were related to. That way, if something went awry, he knew exactly where to find them. James inspired their devotion by paying big salaries and giving them a small percentage of each crop to either blow or sell. His workers were happy and that made him a little complacent in the past, but he was about to get more involved.

Once J was satisfied that all was well in Woodinville, he drove to the South End to take a serious assessment of the damage he would need to fix at the proposed Silver Spoon locale. He walked through, trying to envision what Will had conveyed when they decided to cop the spot. Thinking about the fixtures and ambience from the original site reinvented here, gave James a sense of nostalgia and he started to get enthusiastic about getting this show on the road. He jumped in the car and headed toward the IHOP location that Will worked at. At this point, the restaurant could likely be up and running in a couple of months, but he would need his cousin's assistance to bring the fantasy to life. It would not be a loss to pay Will a salary while they prepped for the grand opening. He could not wait to see the expression on his relative's face when he told him he could quit his nine-to-five today. James walked up to the front counter and asked for Will, but was surprised to find that he had quit a couple of days ago. That was unlike his cousin to up and leave a job with nothing else lined up. He dialed William's cell phone and got a message saying he was unable to receive calls at this time. He decided to drive by his apartment, only to find it completely empty. When he inquired in the office, he was told that his cousin had come in a couple of days ago, announced he was moving and left the same evening. J was worried about Will but knew he was one of the most responsible people he knew. *He will call sooner or later*, he thought.

It had been a long day and James was happy to pick up his son from daycare. As usual, he stopped at Mrs. Johnson's house first to play with him for a while, feed him, bathe him and tuck him in for the evening. He would be glad when Tanya's ass was out of his house in a couple of days. His son could finally return to his own bed and J could move on with his life. Really putting in a full day's work was something he had not done in months and it was tiresome. He could not wait to get home and unwind. It would be nice to sleep in his bed, but Tanya likely still had it occupied. If that was the case, he would be forced to camp out on the couch another night. He chuckled to himself, thinking he wanted to get a new mattress as soon as she left the premises for good. As he pulled into the driveway, he knew right off the bat something was not right; his candy red S Series was sitting on bricks. It was covered with vulgar names and all of the windows were broken out. He looked inside and saw that the seats had been slashed and the deck had been removed. This car was his baby and seeing it like this almost brought J to tears. He walked toward the front door to find it standing wide open. Rather than just running inside, he jogged back to Asaya's car and retrieved his nine millimeter from the center console. He cautiously made his way into the foyer and surveyed the area. The house was in shambles; the dining room table and coffee tables were shattered on the floor, there were holes in all of the walls and it looked like every single dish in the kitchen had been broken. After checking the downstairs for intruders, he slowly made his way up the spiral staircase and gasped when he entered the room, to find a large pile of his and Asaya's clothing doused in bleach. The chemical odor was so strong; you could barely breathe. He started to back out of the room and leave, but then remembered the most important thing. James ran through the bathroom into the walk- in closet and slid the few clothing items left hanging aside. The safe was wide open and almost empty. There was over a hundred thousand dollars in there and it was all gone, along with his jewelry. The only remaining items were business documents. He figured the ignorant bitch was not smart enough for white-collar crime, so she opted for the easy money. He turned his attention to the side of the closet where Tanya stored her belongings and it was empty. She did not leave a trace of herself. It was as if she had never been there. J punched a hole in the closet wall. He racked his brain about where to go to get his money back, but it dawned on him that he knew nothing about this woman he had let come into his home. He went by the guy's house that she was with when she met him, but he had moved on to the next chick and was amused to see that she had wronged J. No details were given about why he was looking for Tanya, but her ex, Steve, could tell something had gone down. "She got you, too, huh?" he smirked.

Without answering, J went back to his car and headed back home to begin the cleanup process. If he ever ran into that bitch again, he would have her head, but he knew that this was his fault. Over the past week, he had violated multiple rules of the game. He had let Carissa know where Rey's stash spot was and he brought a random broad back to his domain. Unbeknownst to him, he must have inadvertently showed her how to get to his loot. There was a lot of cleanup to do and it was on no one but James Buchanan.

THE AFTERMATH

Asaya woke up with the worst headache after exceeding her drinking limit last night. She did not get drunk, but being tipsy was enough to leave her with a vicious hangover. All of the details about what happened between her and Rey last night came flooding back, and she buried her face in the pillow and screamed, asking herself how she could cross the line like that. She hoped she had not ruined her friendship. She rolled over and grabbed her phone off the nightstand. As usual, there was a plethora of missed calls from James. He had been calling her multiple times every day since she left and she had not responded once. He sent a gang of text messages as well, ranging from threats to apologies. At times, she would start to feel guilty and then she would recall all the nights that she sat up, waiting for his key to turn in the door. To Asaya, it was funny how men could disregard women, but did not know what to do when the tables turned. There was a new message from Rey that read, "Saya, I am sorry about what happened last night. We both had too much to drink and used bad judgment. You are the most important person in the world to me and I do not want to lose you. I would like to forget the incident ever happened and continue our friendship."

She did not know how to take what Rey had said. On one hand, she was happy that the slip-up would not damage what they shared, but she felt sad about the fact that he just wanted to forget it ever happened. She wondered if it was a bad experience for him, and whether he was disgusted by her, or just upset at how she left him. Although she thought she had overstepped her boundaries, she could not get the images of his tongue sliding over her lips and neck and his hands roaming all over her body out of her head. Her panties got wet as she recalled the sensuous tango their mouths had done together. She texted him back, "I agree, Rey. I value our friendship and would like to get things back to normal, too. TTYL."

Asaya called her mother to check in on her and Little J, only to find she just missed him. Nothing made her day go better than speaking to her son, so calling too late put a damper on her mood. Knowing that her mom had everything under control made up for it though. Annette told her about everything she had done with her grandson since they last spoke and how pumped he was about returning to daycare today. Then Mrs. Johnson switched gears and her tone was serious. "Hey baby... I have something to talk to you about," her mother started. She was nervous now, because any time a conversation started like that, it was sure to be bad news. She continued, "James was over here yesterday and... I told him I had heard from you and you were fine—"

"Mom! I didn't want him in my business!" Asaya interrupted.

"I did not tell him anything other than that. Now listen here, it ain't right to just let anybody, especially your husband, believe something might have happened to you. I told him you were okay, but needed time." Annette finished. Asaya knew her mom was right. Mrs. Johnson went on to update her about everything that had taken place since yesterday morning. She reluctantly let her know that J had a woman living in the house, and that he had given her a deadline to move out. Unexpectedly, Asaya's eyes filled with tears. She was at a loss for words, knowing that J had committed the ultimate disrespect.

In all the years that they had been together, never once had he let any side chick know where they lived. She could not imagine ever staying there again, knowing someone else had been in her bed. She sat there in silence and her mother interjected, "Saya, you still there? Are you okay?"

"Yes, Mom. I'm fine. Go on," she answered.

Annette went on to tell her about how Carissa jacked No Holds Barred and J let it happen. Asaya wondered why Rey had not mentioned any of this to her. She understood the part about Tanya being at the house. He strongly believed it was out of pocket to dry snitch on another man to his girl. Because he was friends with both of them, Rey knew exactly what James was up to at all times, but would never share any of the details with Asaya. He would be there for her and give her advice, but always stopped short of selling J out or telling her to leave him. However, he did tell her a couple of months back that she should stop sleeping with him because, "ain't no telling what diseases he would pick up from these hoes." After receiving the current events from her mom, she said goodbye and hung up the phone. She sat there on the edge of the bed, feeling stupid for staying loyal to such a selfish person. Last night she could have made love to the man of her dreams; someone she had been in love with her entire life. She had stopped short out of empathy for James Buchanan. She decided that from now on she would not be considering him in any decisions she made. She would do what made her and her baby happy. Asaya threw on her clothes and rushed downstairs to meet Lisa and the other ladies for group fitness.

Rey read the text back from Saya over and over. When he sent the text telling her he wanted to forget it all happened, he hoped her reaction would be to profess her love to him and tell him she wanted to be his wife and have his babies. *So much for fairy tales,* Rey thought. She wished it never happened and wanted to wipe it from her memory. His feelings were hurt but he had already known what kind of lady Asaya was. He should have expected her to show respect to her marriage, even if her other half didn't. She could pretend to have selective amnesia, but there was no way he could forget the images of her in the red bikini or the taste of her tongue in his mouth or the sensation of her ass in the palm of his hands while she rocked back and forth on his dick. He decided to go for a run on the beach to clear his head. He spent the remainder of the day doing some reading and managing his affairs back home long distance. He spoke with his lawyer and found out that the chances of getting No Holds Barred back up and running were slim to none. He was aware this would likely be the case and had already mentally prepared himself to let it go. He also spoke with his housekeeper to make sure everything at home was status quo. His condo was being occupied by an associate and they had no problems to report, so he was cool. When evening arrived, Rey figured it was time he stopped avoiding the situation with J and got down to business. Like Asaya, he had missed several phone calls from him and needed to finally touch base. The phone barely rang before

James picked up, eager to fix the wrong he had done. "Man, Rey. My bad, my nigga. I fucked up, but I plan on making it up. I will get you back every dime you lost, bro. You're my guy and I do not want us to have a problem."

It was not in Rey's personality to let such a huge loss go without some physical punishment, but this had been his boy since they were knee high to a grasshopper. It wasn't like he could just kill him. He accepted the apology and listened as James went over all of the crazy things going on. He told him about the situation with Tanya and it did not surprise Rey at all. Leave it to James to stop worrying about his missing wife and move a rat head into the house.

"Man, you had that coming. Why would you bring her ass to your house?" he asked.

"Shit, another bad decision on my part. Aye, can you put the word out with your people to track her down? She gotta pay for this."

Rey agreed to have everyone on the lookout for the thief and advised J to get his mind off these broads, and on his hustle and his kid. J knew he was right and promised to be more engaged in things that mattered. Rey heard him, but would bet money that it would not be long before J found himself in another fucked up situation. James was so concerned with being forgiven and his own story, he failed to ask any questions about Rey's whereabouts and Rey liked it that way. He hated having to lie to anybody but the police.

Returning to her room after another long day, Asaya looked at the clock. It was 9:46 pm and she knew she would be up late, thinking about her life. Back home at times like this, Rey would talk to her for hours until she fell to sleep, but she did not know if it was too soon after their episode to talk to him. She had thought about him every minute of every second that day. Lisa asked her repeatedly if everything was alright, because she was not participating as much as she usually did. Her counseling session about being accountable for her own happiness and forgiving people that had wronged her got her attention. It was like Lisa was a psychic and could see everything that she was going through; from the crumbling marriage, to the secret short- lived love affair with Rey. She had spent so much time trying to be a good, respectable wife and mother and pleasing other people, she forgot about what she needed. Reflecting on the lesson, she picked up the phone and called her best friend. The phone rang several times and just when Asaya started to think calling was a bad idea, Rey picked up. "Hey, how are you?" he greeted her.

"I'm good," she replied, "Did I wake you?"

"Uh... Do me a favor and quit acting weird. You know

I'm a vampire!" he joked and they both started laughing. *Thank goodness, he knew how to break the ice and fix an awkward exchange,* she thought. They talked until after midnight about what he read today and about how his ventures were going. The only thing he omitted was that he had spoken to her husband and the tragedy regarding their house. He did not want to hide things from her, but he was not trying to alarm her either. As long as baby J was safe, there was no need to put her mind back on her dilemmas at home. She told him about her excruciating workout this morning and how sore her muscles were. He thought about offering to massage them, but instead asked if she wanted to use his hot tub.

"Um... I think I'll pass," she shot back. They started laughing again and finally said goodnight. Their old vibe was back and any tension from yesterday was alleviated. They both fell sound asleep without a care in the world.

As James assessed the destruction and began the cleaning process that evening, he was already planning on how to replace all of the property Tanya destroyed. He had insurance on the car and even had a good policy on the house and everything in it. The only thing that would not be replaced was his money. He was thankful for the reimbursements, but would like nothing more than to wipe

Tanya's gold digging ass off the face of the earth. The time would come and when it did, he would make her suffer the consequences of crossing him. His phone rang from a private number; it was customary for him to let those go to voicemail. But with the complications he was having these days, curiosity got the best of him. "Yo?" he greeted as he hit the send button.

"Hey cuddy, it's me, Will," the caller responded.

"Will! What's up with you, man? I been by your job and your place looking for you today. I had some good news for you this morning, but now I got a big obstacle, so that shit is on hold," James explained. He had already planned to deal with the backlash of yet another setback for The Silver Spoon. He was bewildered by Will's nonchalant response to the update on the status of his restaurant. He said it was cool and told J to take his time and not to sweat it too hard. J was apprehensive about this newfound calm his cousin had discovered. Just last week he was sending text messages about how lazy J was and now he was not tripping. He grilled Will about leaving his job and abandoning his apartment. His explanation was that he had found a better paying gig up in the north end and that he moved in with his girl.

"Your girl? I didn't even know you had a girl," J teased.

Evidently, Will did not find it funny and rushed his cousin off the phone, promising to stay in touch.

STATUS QUO

Thank God, it was Friday! It only took J three days to get his house back in order. He had gotten new furniture and had all of the damage to the walls repaired. The carpet in his bedroom had to be replaced, because the bleach had soaked through and ruined it. He got rid of the bed that Tanya had lain in, because he wanted to fumigate or dispose of anything she had contact with. When Asaya returned, he wanted to be able to be honest with her for the first time and show her that he had fixed all the shit he fucked up. He could not replace her clothing because he did not know where to get everything and was unsure of what size she wore, but he had a bundle of hundred-dollar bills put aside to give her for a shopping spree as soon as she walked in the door. His car would be in the shop again for a while to reconstruct all of the custom fixtures to their former glory. Before he could bring his son back to the house, he changed the locks and installed a state-of-the-art security system that was harder to crack than Fort Knox. Mrs. Johnson was aware of all the obstacles James was facing and was instrumental in dealing with the movers and construction workers that worked on the home. He was forever in her debt because despite what she felt about his misguided moves, she regarded him in a considerate manner. James was sure it was only out of concern for Little J, but it was still something she did not have to do. He had picked his son up from the center and it was nice to pull up in his driveway with his baby. The only thing that was missing was Asaya, and once he got her back, he would not blow his second chance.

Asaya hugged Lisa and said goodbye to the other women in her group. This weekend, there were no activities planned so she had forty-eight hours to be with Rey. "Shit!" she admonished herself for thinking about being with him all weekend. They had not seen each other since Sunday, but had talked each other to sleep every night since. Somehow, all of the conversation they had made her feel closer to him than she already was. She looked forward to getting back in the room, getting comfortable, and lying in bed while they chatted away. They talked a lot before this vacation but it was usually him counseling her. Now that she was away from those issues, she found herself smiling more than she ever had in life and their talks were fun and uplifting. Once in a while, one of them would accidentally slip into being flirtatious, especially late at night, but it was not that big a deal because it was only talking.

After showering and changing into some booty shorts

she would only wear in the house and a fitted tank top, she dialed Rey's number. He did not pick up, so she assumed he was still out and about. As soon as she hung up, there was a knock at the door. She skipped over and looked out the peephole, and could only see red. Snatching the door open, she realized the red was actually a bouquet of roses, accented with some baby's breath. She pushed the bouquet down a little to reveal Rey's flawless face, grinning from ear-to-ear. He handed her the flowers and she invited him in. "Thank you, Rey! They are so pretty!" she exclaimed.

Everybody who knew anything about Asaya knew she loved fresh flowers. James used to get them for her all the time when he was putting his bid in, but as soon as she gave in, the flowers stop coming, along with the attention. She put them in a vase and set them by the window to try to preserve them as long as possible. Rey sat on the couch watching her flutter around the room, glowing because of the small gift he had given her. If it were up to him, he would pick up the things she loved every day. He recalled countless times he had thought about her when he came across her favorite things during shopping excursions, but he would always consider how improper that might look to her man. He was not bothered by James' annoyance, but he suspected his boy was a member of the slap-a-ho tribe and did not want to subject Saya to any more strife than she was already forced to entertain.

"I am going down on the boardwalk for dinner and wanted to invite you," he said.

Without thinking about it, Asaya answered, "Yes! I need to put on some clothes first, though."

"What's wrong with what you have on?" Sensing that she was bashful about exposing so much flesh, he chided, "You ain't dressed no different than anybody on the beach. Let's go."

Asaya reluctantly grabbed her purse and walked out with Rey. As they walked along the beach toward the boardwalk, he tried not to notice that her little aqua blue shorts put her delicious cakes on full display, or that the thin white tank top and unpadded bra she wore exhibited the outline of her breast and nipples. She was practically naked and he suddenly regretted giving other men access to something he coveted. She kept on talking, oblivious to the lust-filled battle he was fighting with himself.

They dined at the Crab Basket and dinner consisted of a large serving of surf 'n' turf. The meal was followed by cocktails and live entertainment. Hawaiian luau girls pranced around the room as the band played folk music. There was even a hip-hop group that performed and

Asaya drug Rey to the dance floor where they C-walked and twerked—at least he watched her twerk. Before they knew, it was after midnight and time to make their way back to the resort. Asaya had drunk a little bit more than she meant to, so she hooked her arm around Rey's to steady herself for the trek back. When they arrived at the lobby of their temporary home, both of them stood there, unsure of what should happen next. He looked at her and asked, "You want to come upstairs and watch a movie?" His mouth said he wanted to watch television, but the way his eyes studied her breasts, she suspected the movie offer was just lip service. He licked his lips the way he did when something or someone had whet his appetite. Asaya could feel heat where his gaze was planted and her nipples instantly got hard.

She lowered her eyelids and replied, "Yes." The yes seemed to apply to a lot more than a movie date. They did not utter a word as the elevator took them to the top floor.

Rey opened the door and ushered Asaya inside. She kicked off her heels and by the time that he looked up from removing his shoes, she was standing so close to him that his face almost landed into the apex between her thighs. He rose slowly, taking in every inch of her until they came face-to-face. He did not have to choose his next move, because it was her turn to be aggressive. She moved forward a few inches and licked his bottom lip before biting it and finally pulling in into her mouth. Even if he wanted to protest, resistance was futile. His phallus promptly became so erect that it hurt. He wrapped his arms around her waist and glided them over her ass to scoop her up; she automatically enclosed his midsection with her legs. He turned around and positioned Asaya against the front door, sticking his tongue deeper and deeper into her mouth. The sexual chemistry was so intense; there was no way on earth either of them could hold back this time. They devoured each other's mouths for what seemed like an eternity, before Rey turned once again and carried Asaya to his California king bed. He deposited her gently and eased over the top of her to kiss her once again. After he got another taste, he moved down and grabbed one of her breasts in each hand. He had wanted to touch them all night and his yearning was so strong, he took one in his mouth through her tank top. That only made him want to feel her skin even more. He pulled the shirt over her head and then reached underneath her to unsnap the bra, looking into her face the whole time. She was amused to find him so fascinated by her. He stared down at her bare chest for a moment, squeezing her titties like he was in the supermarket looking for the best piece of fruit. Asaya squirmed in anticipation. He leaned down and circled one of her nipples with his tongue and she let out a sharp breath. He spent the next few minutes greedily sucking her breast, and just when she was lamenting about that being the best she had ever experienced, he slid his wet tongue down her stomach and stopped to tickle her belly button. By now, Asaya was gyrating like he was already inside of her. He slid her shorts and panties off in one quick gesture and his mouth watered at the sight of her pussy. It was clean-shaven with a landing strip and to him, her clit favored a chocolate-covered cherry; he wondered if it tasted like it looked. Rey timidly licked it to gauge her reaction before continuing. She shivered like a gust of cold air had blown through the room. He went on, making out with her pussy in the same manner he excavated her mouth. He slurped and suckled her hot spot, sticking one finger in and out until Asaya felt herself explode like a volcanic eruption. Rey could feel her pulsating, but kept going until she felt like she could take it no longer and pushed him away. He stood up and slowly dropped his pants and his boxers while Asaya gawked in admiration at his massive manhood. J was doubtlessly well-endowed, but what Rey was working with even put him to shame. He lowered his body and massaged her clit with his phallus to be sure it was wet and ready for entry.

Finding it soaked and slippery, he gradually entered her. "Damn, baby... it's so tight," he whispered near her ear. His warm breath on her ear made her squirt and the sudden rush of moisture caused him to slip further in. He stroked her over and over, until they both came and he collapsed on her in a sweaty heap.

Asaya squinted when she opened her eyes. The sunlight gleaming through the windows from every direction reminded her that she was in Rey's penthouse suite, and not her modest condo downstairs. Last night seemed like an erotic dream that she expected to wake up from this morning. But she was really here and she had really gone all the way with her best friend. Asaya was not sure what was supposed to happen next, and rolled over to see if Rey was still sleeping beside her. He had already gotten up and out of the bed and she became alarmed, wondering if he left because he had made a mistake. Before she could ponder all of the possibilities, he walked into the bedroom with a tray and sat on the edge of the bed next to her. He carefully placed the meal over Asaya's lap and smiled widely at her. "Good morning, sleeping beauty," he greeted her.

"Good morning," she replied. She marveled at the

delicious meal he had prepared. There was French toast, scrambled eggs, turkey bacon and grits. It reminded her of when she and Rey's parents would treat them to a meal after church on Sundays at The Silver Spoon. They spent so much time together back then; it was only natural that their parents became good friends. They would get together on holidays and attend every event that the children were involved in. "Are you gonna eat, too?" she asked.

"Of course." he answered, walking toward the kitchen to grab his tray. They spent the morning watching various local shows and chatting. Rey could tell Asaya was unsure about how to interact with him. She was the only one that was confused; he knew exactly what he wanted and would do whatever it took to get it. He felt it was destiny that he and Saya be together. He hated that he had to snake his boy to get his woman, but at this point, if it was not about his family, his finances or his future wife, he was not concerned. When the time was right, he would address J like a man and let him know that his time with Saya was up and he would prefer that they all be cool. The ideal situation would be for James to listen to logic and move onto his life with the next broad; he was doing it anyway. There was always the possibility that he would trip and want to go to war, but both men knew J would surely lose that battle. Rey did not want to pressure Asaya to be with him, because he knew she would naturally make her next choice her best choice. For now, he would bide his time and show Asaya what it felt like to really be put on a pedestal. He had two weeks left on this island to convince her that she needed to be his. Rey called the front desk and extended his stay two more weeks, and contacted the airlines to reschedule his departure. For the remainder of their stay, he took Asaya shopping, zip lining and even to a salsa class. They proudly held hands everywhere they went and spent any time they were inside, making passionate love to one another. The last few months they had both been abstinent were well worth the wait.

BLOOD IS THICKER THAN MUD

James waved goodbye to his son and Mrs. Johnson as he pulled away from her house. He had spent Friday night cooking dinner and dessert for his son and they ate and watched cartoons until they both passed out. He agreed to drop him off with his grandmother Saturday morning for a day at the local waterpark. He would head out to Woodinville later today after he rode through the South End and checked out his peeps in the old neighborhood. He scrolled through his phone methodically and deleted any contacts that had nothing to do with his business or his family as he sat in traffic on I-5. Doing that put into perspective, just how many women he had been dealing with over the last few years. Some of them, he did not even remember, but saw picture messages to and from them indicating that they had carnal knowledge of one another. He chuckled to himself, thinking, *Cocaine is a hell of a drug.* He knew temptation was a problem and wanted to limit contact. J had even gone so far as to reply to messages from women, letting them know that he was married and asking that they lose his digits. It was hard to convince many of them that it was not the wrong number, considering he never gave any indication that he was committed to anyone.

He had also let go of his denial and enrolled in an outpatient treatment program.

He exited the freeway onto Martin Luther King Way South. The sun was beaming in through the sunroof and J was exuberant about the possibilities, and decided to roll past the future location of The Silver Spoon to get a feel for what kind of potential patrons frequented the area during the weekend. As he turned onto Rainier Avenue, he nodded at several of his old comrades standing on the corner. He shook his head at the revelation that they were still doing the exact same thing they all did as teens. He was thankful that he learned to survive and had a hunger for greatness early on in life. A couple of them tried to wave him down, hoping to get a ride here or there, but J kept it moving. Gone were the days when any old person could jump in with him, just because they happened to live in the same neighborhood as kids. Some would say he was acting brand new, but he knew that any sensible person with something to lose knew these dudes messed around with that wet, and ain't no telling what crazy shit they might be on.

As James pulled up to the spot, he was taken aback by a full construction crew hard at work on the renovation project. He swooped into the parking lot and jumped out of the car, eager to find out what the hell was going on. He ran up to the first worker he saw and asked that he be directed to the foreman. He was directed to a tall slim white guy standing in front of the restaurant, barking orders at everyone else. J confronted him without even offering a greeting. "Hey, what's going on here? Who authorized you to start construction here?"

The man gave him a blank stare as if he did not understand English and replied, "The owner did. Who are you?" James thought he must have misheard him, because he knew damn well he did not sign any contract with any company to start anything. Will could not possibly have hired anyone, because he needed J's money to do so.

He angrily responded, "I am the owner!"

"Well, according to this paperwork, I show the owner as William Buchanan and I happen to have met him, so I know you are not him." James snatched the contract the foreman was showing him and reviewed it. It certainly looked like Will's signature and because the property was under his name, J could do nothing to intervene. He picked up his phone to call Will, but remembered he had no current contact information for him. He dialed his uncle, William Sr., to see if he had seen him, but he seemed to have dropped off the face of the earth. It was unclear what was going on, but James fully intended to get to the bottom of it today.

Looking through his contacts, James stopped on one labeled "INCOGNITO". This was his go-to guy any time he needed to track someone down, although up to this point, he had yet to provide any credible leads as to where Carissa had vanished to. She'd never existed in any public records, so J surmised that it was a set-up from the jump. Anxious to find out what Will was up to, J started talking before the man even said hello. "Yo, this is J. I need your services right this second." The private investigator knew the money would be right, so he agreed to meet J right away for details. Within half an hour, he was pulling into the vacant parking lot and was provided information on the suspicious circumstances surrounding J's little cousin's moves. He also noted all of the information from the construction worker's vehicles, in case it was helpful in his search. To occupy his mind until he got the answers he was looking for, J went on to Woodinville and spent a few hours inspecting the plants and going through the stack of mail on the desk in his office. Just when he was about done, his phone rang and "INCOGNITO" flashed on the screen. He answered the line asking, "You got something for me?" he asked. The detective relayed all of the particulars about what he uncovered. He was able to confirm and William Buchanan was the person that solicited and paid the construction company. He also supplied a current address in Bellevue and a new number for Will. James thanked the man for his help and contemplated what his next move would be.

"Bellevue?" he muttered. He asked himself how in the hell Will was living in Bellevue. It was one of the most expensive communities on the outskirts of the town and J knew no cooking job was kicking in like that. He decided calling the new number for Will was not the best idea. Instead, he headed toward I-90 to check out the new residence his cousin had conveniently forgot to mention.

James pulled into the gated community, scrutinizing the half-million dollar homes lined up one right after the other. He had to have gotten the address wrong, because this was no small apartment. If this was where Will had relocated to, he was living like a boss. J found the correct house number and drove past it, parking at the end of the cul-de-sac. The two-story home sat on a manicured lot and from outside you could tell that the bottom floor was complete with cathedral ceiling and shiny hardwood floors. It looked brand new and had a three-car garage. This spot was about three times the size of James' house and Will was claiming he needed financial help. He pulled out the set of binoculars he had purchased. Through the floor-to-ceiling windows in the living room, he could see Will in the kitchen preparing a meal and decided to knock on the door to ask some questions. As he unstrapped his seatbelt, a red Beamer pulled into the driveway and a woman emerged. J picked up his binoculars to get a closer look. His mouth dropped open as the lady came into view; he knew this chick. It was Carissa. James was so hot, he wanted to walk right up on her, but instead he sat back to see what would happen next. Will came out of the front door smiling, walked up and gave her a hug and a kiss. He then went to the trunk and retrieved some grocery bags. The couple disappeared into the house and J watched for a few more minutes as they unloaded the bags and filled the refrigerator and the cupboards. All the puzzle pieces started to come together; Will quitting his job, leaving his apartment, not tripping about the delay on starting the remodeling. His own family member had set him up. If it were anyone else, there would be no questions asked. He would have kicked in the front door and made them both pay with their lives. But this was his cousin… his first cousin. J had always looked out for him and shot him some ends when he needed it. He financed every brilliant idea Will happened to come up with. J knew Will had to be dealt with. If there was one thing J would not tolerate, it was disloyalty and disrespect. But this situation had to be handled a little differently than any other. He had to handle Will and his new girl without letting a soul know it was on him. It had to be planned carefully and there was no room for error. If anyone in the family got wind that J was behind this, it would tear them apart. He reluctantly put his binoculars in the glove box and sped out of the neighborhood. He had a lot of groundwork to lay before he could get rid of the snakes in his garden.

James rushed to his house and went straight to his bedroom to access the safe in the back of his closet. Since his lapse in judgment with Tanya, he had the safe replaced with a more secure model. There were various security measures he had to go through to open it, including thumbprint recognition. The only way he could be jacked now was if somebody dragged his dead body to the closet. Fortunately, Tanya had neglected to swipe the documents from the safe, along with the other valuables. He pulled the entire stack of papers out and sat on his bed, flipping through them until he found what he was looking for. J and Will had agreed that although Will was the official property owner, the deed would be stored with James. Will was given a second copy in case he needed to handle any property matters. With the deed in hand, James contacted his lawyer. "Mr. Dawson. How are you? This is James Buchanan." He introduced himself.

"Oh... James. How are you, son? Long time; no hear. What can I do for you today?" Mr. Dawson inquired. Clarence Dawson was a long-time friend of James' grandfather and whenever there were any legal matters that needed an expert opinion or representation, he was J's man. Overall, Mr. Dawson was a pretty stand-up guy, but because of their history, he was willing to bend the law a little for James. They went over what was going on with the newly acquired property and Mr. Dawson went over a process by which James could snatch the real estate from right under his cousin's nose. Naturally, the seasoned attorney pretended not to be aware that any signatures of Will's would come by way of forgery. He assured James that by Monday morning, he would send him the warranty deed necessary to register the restaurant under his name.

His next call was to his old school partner, Benji. He was one of the hood's hot boys; always in the midst of a white-collar crime ring, but never careless enough to get caught. He would work miracles with minimal information. Any time J came across a name, birth date and social security number, he would pass it along to Benji and before he knew it, the victim's bank accounts had been emptied. He would even withdraw a target's retirement funds if they had any. He would give J a generous

143

percentage of any money he got, so he could profit from the lick without getting directly involved. His plan was to recover what he could from the debacle at No Holds Barred before disposing of Will and Carissa. Knowing his cousin, he blew some of the money on tricking with low budget broads, cars, and living above his means in that expensive rental property, but his frugal ass more than likely put that majority of it away for a rainy day. As it turned out, when the detective tracked down Will, he was able to finally identify the woman he knew as "Carissa" and give him all of her background information. Benji wrote down everything he needed and got to work finding out where the two lovebirds stored their money.

It was getting late and James called Mrs. Johnson to see how she and JJ had fared at the water park. They were just leaving to head home and he had so much fun, he was knocked out in his car seat. They both thought it best that he just stayed with his grandmother for the evening. After hanging up, he laid back to assess all the shit that had happened to him lately. He did not even recognize that he had drifted off to sleep when he was awakened by the ringing of his phone. "Mrs. Buchanan" was displayed on the screen. James was apprehensive about answering, not wanting to say the wrong thing and aggravate her.

"Hello?" he answered.

"Hey, James, it's Asaya," she answered, holding her breath in anticipation of him going off and cussing her out.

Instead, his tone was soft and he replied, "I know. How are you?" Shocked by what seemed like concern for her, she told him she was fine and went on to explain that she had gone on a retreat, but stopped short of disclosing her location. He let her know that he understood why she had to leave and was not upset with her. Asaya rolled her eyes at his suggestion that she gave a fuck what made him mad. James was tempted to tell her everything that had happened over the past two weeks, how he had changed his ways and was ready to be a real husband to her, but he thought he should take things slow instead. The talk was brief and he was still unclear on when she was coming back. Asaya said goodbye and before she hung up, he stopped her. "Asaya. I just wanted to say I'm sorry." he pleaded. She was thrown off by his apology. He never apologized for anything in all the years she knew him.

"For what?" she asked sarcastically.

"Everything," he clarified. There were a few seconds of silence before they both disconnected the line. James lay there looking up at the ceiling before finally falling back to sleep. Asaya did not know what to make of the phone call.

For some reason, she felt guilty for leaving without saying anything and for cheating on J. She shook off her remorse and exited her room to join Rey in the penthouse for dinner and a movie.

ONE MAN'S TRASH

Tanya sat on the balcony of her temporary residence, taking in the sprawling industrial view. The condominium was beautiful and everything in it was expensive and top of the line. The only thing she did not like was the view. Instead of mountains, trees or lakes, the unit overlooked an area with various warehouses and industrial complexes. At least there was a telescope pointing skyward, so she could view the stars and moon at night. Tanya wanted to be somewhere peaceful where she could just be alone with the sound of nature, but ever since she fucked up James' shit, she did not dare leave the house until she had an airtight plan to keep him off her ass. Having associates in high places meant she had somewhere comfortable to hole up when things got sticky, but there was nothing like being in the house with a man you loved and playing wifey. She looked around, wondering why someone who could afford any place they wanted posted up here with all the pollution floating around. "I guess he got his reasons," Tanya mumbled to herself. She traipsed back through the slider into the living room and plopped down on the couch. She picked up her big, black Michael Kors bag off the coffee table and emptied the contents onto the couch. She ran her hand over the bundles of cash and the expensive jewelry, wondering if it was all worth it. She had always been the same way; if a man was going to throw her out like yesterday's garbage, she would make sure she left with something. Usually she had no qualms about jacking some punk ass trick, but this time was different. Tanya actually had feelings for James and doing something to hurt him felt wrong. Yes, she knew he was an asshole... a married asshole, but he had taken her in and let her see what it was like to be in the upper echelon... at least briefly. There were no lavish shopping sprees or trips with the money she took from his safe. She had not spent a dime because she was not sure she wanted to keep it. Getting him like this was not really her idea anyway; her business associate and constant advisor gave her the suggestion, as he tended to do from time to time, and she just followed instructions. The fear and regret was like a rock in the bottom of her stomach as she tried to come up with a way of fixing this. She would let the man of the house know she wanted to make amends with James when he got back tomorrow, and ask what her next move should be.

James hugged Mrs. Johnson as he left with Little J to head home for the evening. They had just eaten another one of her delectable meals, and were ready to get home and get comfortable. Everything had pretty much gone back to normal over the last couple of weeks since Tanya vandalized the house and robbed the safe. The only things out of place were his situation with his boy, Rey, and his relationship with Asaya. J had been talking to her on a daily basis; she let him know that she would be returning to Seattle in a few days. Things were so different from the way they were a month ago and he did not know what to expect when his wife returned. He had made progress in changing while she was gone. He had also made numerous attempts at reaching out to his boy, but Rey would rarely respond. J decided to let it go for now and focus on other things. Most of his time was spent at the warehouse tending to his plants, with his son, or at his mother-in-law's house. Over the past few weeks, James and Annette had grown closer and it was a good feeling being treated like he was one of the family once again. To him she was a nosey, know-it-all, overbearing, potty mouth woman, but she was also forgiving and caring toward the people she loved. That explained why she turned on him so quick when he turned on her daughter. Now that things were back to normal, he would make sure he never let it get dysfunctional again. The medical marijuana business was in full swing and completely under wraps; he had lost a lot when he got jacked, but was able to recover most of it when Benji had located and emptied every bank account Will and his shady boo had. Of the half-million dollars they stole, he was able to recoup almost four hundred racks. He never let on that his cousin was the perpetrator or that he had gotten back the funds to Rey, because he was not sure he wanted to hand over that much cheese after all the work it took to get it back. The only loose ends left on the No Holds Barred situation were Will and Carissa, and J would make sure they were taken care of before Asaya got back. That way, he would have no distractions.

Asaya embraced Lisa for a long time before letting her go. They had spent the last month together and it would be hard not seeing her any more. The ladies exchanged personal information and promised to keep in touch. Asaya walked Lisa to the lobby and waved goodbye as she disappeared into a taxicab. She, on the other hand, would have a couple of additional days in paradise, because her flight did not leave until late Sunday night. Two more nights together and a wake up, and everything would change once again between her and Rey. She took the elevator to the top floor and knocked on his door. He answered with no shirt on and immediately, Asaya's panties got wet. "Why you still knocking?" he asked jokingly. He grabbed her hand and pulled her to him, closing the door behind her. He gave her one of those desperate, deep kisses that made her believe he could not live without her. When they finally pulled themselves apart, he led her to the couch and sat down next to her. It was almost like they had lived together for the past couple of weeks. The only time they were not together was during her retreat activities and immediately after. When she would return to her room, she would shower and spend time talking to James on the phone before joining Rey. Asaya thought she had it all figured out after she hooked up with Rey the first few times. She would return home, grab her belongings-or whatever was left of them, take her son and leave James' ass. She had not planned to move in with Rey immediately, but it was bound to happen soon. That had all changed since she started having nightly conversations with J. He seemed to be a completely different person, like he was when she first met him, only... better. He was everything she wished he had been all these years, attentive, humble, appreciative and a good dad. But Asaya was no idiot. Although she had never experienced it before, she knew that when a woman finally gets the nerve to leave her no-good man, he usually pulls out all the stops to get her back, only to go right back to the way he was when she returns. Nevertheless, Asaya was confused as to what the right thing to do was. She glanced over at Rey and considered how happy he looked. He had laid it all on the table, how he had always loved her and dreamed about being with her; that he wanted to take care of her and Little J for the rest of his life. It was all too much to take in. She had gone from feeling alone and isolated to being pursued by two men at once. Her heart raced at the thought of having to disappoint someone she loved.

James was awakened Saturday morning by a pounding on his front door. He grabbed his pistol and tiptoed down the stairs and to the front door. It was just before dawn and he was not expecting company, so he was not taking any chances, especially after the way Tanya caught him slipping. He looked through the peephole to see Will pacing back and forth on his front porch impatiently. He thought about just blasting his turncoat cousin through the door, but knew there was no way to justify an impulsive move like that. He opened the door a crack and Will eagerly pushed his way in. James stepped back looking at his cousin for answers and preparing to put him down if he needed to. But Will seemed oblivious to the ire his older relative was directing at him. "Cuddy, man, I need you! I got a big problem," he cried with a pleading look in his eyes.

"What's going on?" James asked flatly.

"I been stacking my checks for a minute and saving them and somebody hit my account. Now I got rent coming up that I can't pay and a car note," he explained. James stared at Will, wondering when it got this easy to tell a bold-faced lie. There was a lease payment to make, but he had bought both cars with cash. What he really needed was money to keep his Silver Spoon dreams alive.

"How much you need to hold?" he asked, pretending to be concerned.

"Man… at least ten racks, cuddy. When the restaurant is up and running, I'll get it right back to you," he begged.

"I ain't even got it like that, cousin. But I do have a move for you where you can get that and a little more. Come back by this evening and I got you," he promised. James watched as Will jumped in the scarlet red Beamer that "Carissa" had been driving when she pulled up at the house in Bellevue. He knew that as soon as times got tough, his weak ass cousin would bring his ass to him begging for a kick down. Everything was going according to plan and at this rate, the traitor would be out of his life permanently before tomorrow morning.

He picked up his phone and dialed a number he rarely ever called. A male on the other end of the line answered,

"Yeah."

"He's on the way back," James stated and hung up.

The man sat at the end of the cul-de-sac waiting. Will sped into the driveway and went inside. Within five minutes, the front door swung open and "Carissa" came storming out with a purse on one arm and a duffle bag over her shoulder. Will was holding onto her arm in an attempt to get her to stay, but she was not having it. She was yelling at the top of her lungs about how broke he was and how he had lost all of their money. The man watching shook his head at the scene. J told him that Will was a pushover, but the sight of him in that yard begging a worthless gold-digger to stay made the man ill. She held out her hand, ordering him to hand over the car keys. He refused to hand them over and she gave up and stomped off down the street, deciding she did not need anything else from him. When she got to the corner, she turned around one last time to flip him off before making her exit. Will tried to warn her but it was too late... A dark SUV jumped the curb and hit Carissa, sending her flying through the air. Her contorted body lay on the grass covered in blood. Hearing the screeching of tires, several residents ran outside to investigate the commotion. Will covered his mouth and gingerly backed into the front door, closing it softly behind him. The man in the car pulled out of the cul-de-sac and around the crowd.

James checked the time on his watch again. It was 7:30 pm and Will still had not arrived at his place. He was beginning to think the plan needed to be revised when his cousin appeared at the door. He looked like something the cat had drug in. His eyes were puffy and swollen, and he looked stressed. James asked him, "You okay, Will?"

"Yeah, I'm cool," Will lied. They jumped in Will's car, but J requested that he drive since he would be waiting in the car once they got to their destination. J reached over his shoulder and placed the small carrier on the backseat. He went over the order of events once again. Will would walk into the location, hand the people inside the carrier; they would give him some cash and he would return to the car, simple as that. As they pulled up to the spot, James started to second-guess himself, but there was no way he could let someone get away with what his cousin had done.

Will took the bag and entered through a side door. Once inside, he handed it over to the man as he was supposed to. The man sat the bag on the table and pulled out the contents. Alarm washed over William Buchanan's face when he realized the only thing his bag contained was a couple of bricks *and not the kind he was expecting*. He wanted to run back out the door he came in, but he knew it was useless. Outside, James heard the faint sound of a small caliber weapon being fired twice. He drove off into the dusky evening, sipping on the bottle of Hennessy he had brought with him. Tears ran down his face and he tried to push the thought of what he had just done out of his mind.

It was Sunday morning and Rey's flight was leaving at noon. He hated leaving the resort and facing the reality back in Seattle. If it were up to him, he would spend the rest of his life here, laying on the beach with Saya and making love to her. He could never get sick of the taste of her body. Asaya walked him to the Town Car waiting in the hotel drive. They hugged for what seemed like forever and he asked her what she would do when they got home. Up to this point, he had beat around the bush, but now it was time for hard decisions. "I'm going to go see JJ and my mom and then talk to James so we can move forward." She answered; unsure she even believed everything she was saying.

Rey aggressively held her head between his hands and looked into her eyes with a cold expression. "Look Saya, you know how I feel about you. I offered to take care of you, treat you right and even treat your son like my own. Do not play with me," he warned. The sweet, romantic Rey was gone and this one was intimidating and scary. She nodded her head nervously and he kissed her hard on the mouth before riding off toward the airport. As she watched her lover ride away, Asaya started crying because he knew she had probably just made the worst mistake of her life. She came to Hawaii to clear her head and ended up making the situation more complicated than ever.

As Rey sat on the plane, mentally preparing for the long flight home, he thought about James Buchanan. He had intended on forgiving him for the loss of the club and the stack, but after Benji let him in on the details about Will and Carissa, it became clear that J had found out who got him and had gotten the money back. It appeared he had no intention of telling him what went down or replacing the five-hundred thousand dollars he had recovered. When Rey first heard about it, he waited for J to call, give him back the money and plead for forgiveness on behalf of Will. But instead he kept the money and smoked his own family member. Rey was feeling no remorse for fucking his wife and would feel none when he took her and J's son away. If he was not loyal to his own blood, Rey would never expect J to hold him down. In his opinion, people like James Buchanan were snakes and needed to be exterminated.

A FAMILY AFFAIR

Tanya perked up when she heard a key turning in the lock. She had been cooped up in this unfamiliar apartment for two whole weeks and could use some company. There were only so many talk shows and reality shows you could watch before you went stir crazy. She grabbed her bowl off the table and ran into the kitchen to wash it in an attempt to clean up before he opened the door. He kept his place in impeccable condition and she did not want to have anything out of order when he arrived. The front door slammed shut and she could hear his footsteps walking across the floor toward the kitchen. "Aye, what's up, girl?" he greeted as he stood in the doorway.

She turned around and looked at him, taking in his statuesque body and his flawless features. Reyhan Lucas was the most beautiful, sexy, perfect specimen of manhood that she had ever laid her eyes on. "Hey, Rey." She blushed. She dried her hands and walked over to give him a hug. He patted her on the back, careful to keep sufficient space between them. They both went to the living room and sat on the couch to catch up. She tried to make casual conversation about his business trip and how it went, but he was not interested in sharing. Instead, he started grilling her about the goings on with James and her. After J told her to kick rocks, she made a frantic phone call to Rey, needing guidance and assistance. He told her to take the items from the safe, leave, and stay hidden in his apartment until he returned. She was hurt by James' callous behavior, so the destruction of the house was her own idea.

Tanya started to tell him about how much she missed J and wanted to make it right. He listened to her plight offering to help her get her man back. He knew Asaya would be leaving her husband permanently and he needed someone to occupy James' time until he decided what he would do about him. Getting him to take Tanya back would be tricky. It would take an act of God to get him to leave Saya alone and downgrade to this chick, but with the right game plan, Rey was certain he could make it happen. He advised Tanya to sit back and be patient while he put it together. She gave him her sexiest come-hither look and said, "I don't know how much more patient I can be." Rey shook his head and walked into his bedroom, shutting the door behind him. It seemed that no matter how much he laced Tanya, she could not help being a hood rat. She had approached him on numerous occasions, throwing it at him and he declined every time. When he found out James had his own side hustles going on and didn't intend on including him, he decided whatever bond they shared had been severed. He made J a partner in all of his ventures, even the ones he was not qualified for. Since then, he had slowly starting keeping his ambitions to himself and making big moves solo.

He pulled Tanya aside one day and told her he would pay her to get at J. He knew his friend would take the bait, because he would hit anything with a slit. He started pulling the strings and gradually weaving Tanya into J's life to cause discord between him and Asaya. He was tired of waiting for Asaya to leave James or vice versa and from her long, late night talks, he knew she was ready to make a move. Rey knew what woman he wanted and was ready to take her. He undressed and showered before getting out in the mix. As he exited his bedroom, Tanya was sitting on a barstool near the kitchen. She had changed into a provocative, low-cut blue dress in an attempt to get his attention. Rey made a mental note that she could not have showered before getting dressed, because he was in the only available restroom. Tanya switched across the room and threw her hands around his neck, leaning in to plant a wet one on him. Rey moved to the side, narrowly dodging the bright red lipstick caked on her mouth, and put his hands up to gently nudge Tanya away. She looked down, disappointed by his rejection. Rey grabbed her by the chin and pulled her face up to look at him. "T, you do not need a man's attention to validate you. You need to focus on you and take care of yourself. I love you like a sister, but that's all," he chided her. Tanya nodded her head in agreement and backed away to give Rey room to leave. He gave her a smile on the way out and she responded with a half-hearted grin. After he left, she put on her stilettos and left, on a mission to find her next ex-man. Rey said he would help her get James back, but she learned a long time ago, that you should never trust anything a man tells you. She was not sure what his angle was, but it seemed that Mr. Lucas had his own agenda and it probably would not work out in her best interest.

As Rey cruised down I-5 toward Seattle, he dialed J. Although he was a snake, he needed to be kept in close proximity; that way Rey would know what was going on with him, Tanya, and Asaya at all times. He had not waited all these years to leave his future in the hands of fate. J picked up the phone, surprised to hear from his childhood friend. They agreed to meet at a local Starbucks and catch up. Uncertain about how much Rey knew about everything involving No Holds Barred, James brought his gun, just in case something popped off. He did not think Rey would ever hurt him, but thought he should hope for the best and prepare for the worst. They sat down after ordering coffee and got down to business. He told Rey about the lack of leads in the robbery situation, advised him that it would take quite some time for him to recoup the loss, and gave more detail about what happened with Tanya. Suddenly, his head dropped and he looked to be wiping tears as he notified Rey about the murder of Will. "They found him somewhere out south in an alley... shot twice," he explained. "My cousin didn't deserve this. I'm gonna make whoever did it pay," he vowed.

He saw no need to mention Carissa; Rey did not even know that was not her real name. As he talked about his cousin's unfortunate death, Rey thought about knocking his teeth out, but kept his cool. He really wanted to see if J could duplicate the long distance lies he told him in person. That was the confirmation he needed that he was on track with his thoughts about J. Fortunately, instead of asking detailed questions about his trip, James only asked how it went and left it at that. Rey figured he was too wrapped up in his own self-destruction to be concerned with anyone else. They ended the informal meeting and embraced each other before parting ways.

Asaya exited the terminal at Sea-Tac Airport, looking

around for a cab to flag down. As she surveyed the curbside pickup lane, she saw her car parked there waiting. She did a double take to make sure she was not seeing things. Nope... it was her vehicle with her husband at the wheel. "Shit!" she whispered as she reluctantly walked in the direction of the gold Nissan Altima.

She was not prepared to see him yet and thought she would at least have the cab ride to ready herself. As she approached the car, James just sat there staring for a minute, before he realized this was actually his wife. With that recognition, he hopped out and grabbed her bags, kissing her on the cheek before he placed the bags in the trunk. He ran back to the passenger side, opening the door. Asaya silently sat down, not knowing what she should say. James appeared to be nervous as well, so he asked a couple of questions about her trip and continued to their destination in silence. J felt like he had picked up a complete stranger. His wife looked different. She had obviously been eating right and working out, because she was as small as she was when they met. Her clothing had changed drastically. She had on a fitted leopard-print dress that showed all of her curves and stopped just above the knees with a plunging neckline that made her perky C-cups look as if they belonged in a storefront window. No longer was she drowning in a baggy outfit that hid the extra pounds she had accumulated. Her usual milk chocolate complexion had gotten a few shades darker and appeared to be even smoother. He was used to Asaya pulling her hair back into a boring bun every day, but she had let her shoulder-length, jet-black curls fall freely around her face. She completed the look with a pair of five-inch, black open toe heels and matching chunky jewelry. She had always thought she was a little too tall, so she tended to stick with either flats or super low heels. Yes, this was definitely a new leaf his conservative wife had turned over.

Their first stop was to pick up their son from Asaya's mother. Before they could get out of the car, Mrs. Johnson was all over her daughter, hugging and kissing her, and telling her how beautiful she was before handing over Little J. All of the Johnson brothers even showed up to greet their sister and everyone marveled over the changes in her appearance. Mrs. Johnson had made a meal fit for a king— or in this case, a queen. The family knew James was still mourning the death of William, so they did their best to treat him kindly. After hanging out for a few hours and stuffing themselves, it was getting dark, so the Buchanans got on the road headed home.

After tucking JJ in the bed for the night, Asaya and

James finally had to sit down and face one another. There were no more distractions and the pink elephant in the room needed to be addressed. They sat at the dining room table and he took her by both hands. "Baby, I'm really, really sorry for everything I've done to you. Please forgive me," he pleaded desperately. Asaya tried to look away but he put his hand on her face, forcing her to look into his eyes. "Please?" he asked again. She looked at him and for the first time since meeting him, thought he was genuinely apologetic about hurting her. Before she could answer, he told her he wanted to be completely honest in the future and started by going over everything he had been doing over the past several months, all the way up to Tanya stealing his money and tearing up the house. He stopped short of letting her in on the fact that he had been jacked by his own cousin, and that he had him killed. He was scared that Asaya's wide-eyed expression meant he had done too much to turn back, but she was actually shocked by his confessions. For the most part, she had already known about the affairs, the drugs and all the other violations against their marriage, but to hear him actually admit to them was a stunner. The fact that he was risking everything to do the right thing touched her heart. For the first time in years, he acted as if he loved her and did not want to lose her. Asaya did love James; she always had and always would. His vulnerability made her feel guilty and for a second she thought about telling him that she had been with Rey in Hawaii, but the possibilities of what could come of such betrayal made her reconsider. She told James she still loved him and asked him to give her some time to decide what she wanted to do. Happy for the chance at reconciliation, he gladly obliged. As James slept peacefully next to his wife for the first time in weeks, Asaya tossed and turned all night, wondering how the hell she was going to get out of this mess she had created.

THE CHICKENS COME HOME

Rey walked in and slammed the door hard behind him. Afraid to ask what his problem was, Tanya did not utter a word as he stormed past her into his room, shutting the door. Ever since returning from his business trip, he was not himself. He was always in a horrible mood and kept his phone with him at all times. She tried to comfort him and be a friend, but after being turned away so many times, she just gave him space and waited until his issues blew over. Besides, Tanya had her own problems to deal with and was not going to be stressed by someone else's drama. Rey made it clear that he did not want her in his personal affairs and she minded her own damn business.

It had been a full two weeks since returning from Hawaii and Rey had yet to hear Saya's voice. He had texted her repeatedly and even went as far as to show up at her house unexpected, pretending to be looking for James on a few occasions. If she was home alone, she ignored the door and if her husband was there, she disappeared into her bedroom until Rey left. Asaya had responded one time by text, asking him to stop and saying she would call him soon. Now he was starting to feel like a fool and it was pissing him off. Rey suspected she had changed her mind and decided to stay with her man. He started investigating to make sure his hunch was on point. On weekday mornings Asaya and J would ride together to take their son to daycare. James would drop Asaya at work and Rey would wait in the parking lot at her job, wanting to catch her at lunchtime. But his plans were ruined by the sight of the candy red Mercedes pulling in just before noon to whisk her away for a romantic meal. In the evenings, he would find them at her mother's house, on family outings, or locked up in their home together. Yesterday, he had watched them jogging on a trail by their house together and was crushed when J pinned Saya against a large evergreen tree and made out with her. And this morning, he tracked them to Christ the King Church, holding hands and pretending to be a happy couple. He came to the conclusion that the woman he loved had played him. He angrily recounted how he had put his feelings out there and she used him to make her feel like a real woman. As soon as they were back, she went running back to the dude that fucked her over in the first place. He tossed his phone on the bed and went to the kitchen to get a drink. He needed to snap out of this and figure out how to handle this. He plopped down in the chair and looked over at Tanya. Her eyes were severely swollen and he could tell she had been crying. "T, what's wrong?"

Rey asked.

"I got some bad news, Rey," she replied, sobbing. She reached into her purse and whipped out a sandwich bag with a pregnancy test inside. She handed it over to him and he could clearly make out the plus sign. Rey leaned back in the chair with a sinister grin on his face. Just when he thought all hope was lost, destiny showed up and gave him the lift he needed. *So much for the Buchanan's happily ever after,* he mused. He put the bag on the table, stood up and hugged Tanya as if she had just saved his life. She did not understand why he was so happy, but he assured her that after he told her what he had in store, she would be as ecstatic as he was.

The last two weeks had been the best of Asaya Buchanan's marriage. She was so in love with James, she could not contain it. He had even attended church with her today and all of the fear she had about being embarrassed by him again was unrealized. As a matter of fact, she was pleasantly surprised by how committed he was to the service. He held James Jr. on his lap and held her hand the whole time. He would look at her every time the pastor made a reference to man and wife, to let her know he heard it and was living by it. Everything that happened in Hawaii seemed a lifetime away now and if she could take it back, she would. Rey had been texting her nonstop, with his words ranging from sweet to aggressive and at times, bordering on threatening. Maybe she was paranoid, but there were a few times she swore she saw him driving by the house or sitting outside her mom's. She would have to end things with him sooner than later and she would have to do it in person, because it was the respectful thing to do. Rey had been her best friend all of her life and she did not want to hurt him or lose him, but she could not sacrifice her family to be with him. She bowed her head and prayed he would understand.

After finishing the usual Sunday ritual, James and Asaya lay in the bed talking and laughing together. She had not been with him sexually since returning. She knew he had been living with a woman briefly and was waiting for a clean bill of health from him. She could not tell J that she also wanted to let Rey know what was good, before re-consummating her relationship with him. James agreed to the terms and got a full examination from his doctor. He did not seem to mind spending all of his time with Asaya and not being sexual. They watched a couple of movies while sipping on some red wine and she drifted off into a deep slumber. As Asaya slept, J went to use the restroom. As he washed his hands, he glanced over at the closet door. His wife had yet to fully unpack her belongings and curiosity was getting the best of him about what she was hiding. They had both talked about everything and she had filled him in on the retreat she took part in, but something was bothering him. Some parts of the story just did not fit together and he felt like he was missing something. Unable to control his urge to find out, he went into the closet and unzipped her bag. He sifted through several bathing suits and new clothing that she had failed to mention, but that was small shit. He kept digging and came to the bottom of the bag, where he found a flat box that he would have missed if he were not so observant. He carefully removed the lid from the box and there staring him in the face, was a picture of his so- called best friend, Reyhan Lucas and his wife hugged up on the beach. The way he had his hands all over her body did not look too platonic. James could feel heat coming over his face and spreading over his body like wild fire. He flipped the image over and there was a note to Asaya from Rey:

> *I have loved you since the day I laid eyes on you I*
> *dreamed about making you my queen. And on this*
> *day on a tropical beach*
> *I finally get a chance at realizing my dream*
>
> > *I love you now and forever, Rey*

171

James held his head between his hands, trying to 'un-find' the truth about the woman he loved and the man he had made his closest confidant. He went on digging and found other pictures, gifts from Rey, sexy lingerie that had obviously been worn and even came across a nearly empty box of Magnum condoms. He wanted to walk in the room and choke Asaya to death while she slept, and then beat Rey's face in until he stopped breathing, but instead he dropped to his knees and prayed. He was in disbelief that his wife could do something like this to him. He knew Rey and any other man was capable, but could not believe Asaya would do this. He could not comprehend she could step out on him like this. But he knew the answer; he had abused her love for so long and took for granted that she would never leave him. He had slept on the job and somebody tried to slip in and take his position. He put all of the items back where he found them, and took a minute to calm himself and dry his face. He had not even realized he was crying until that moment. He knew what he had to do. He would forgive his wife. He blamed himself for her transgression; he pushed her into another man's arms. But he would never forgive Rey. He pretended to be a friend for years, only to snake him for his most valuable possession. He had crossed the wrong person and that would cost him his life. J went back to his spot next to Asaya. He looked at her face and recognized that lately she was the happiest he had ever known her to be. She had been good to him ever since he met her. He vowed not to make her pay for getting used as a pawn in a game she did not know she was playing. Asaya rolled over when she heard James moving. "Hey baby. Why you still up? Are you okay?" she asked, sounding groggy.

He smiled down at his wife, kissed her on the forehead and answered, "Yeah, I'm cool, baby. Go back to sleep." Without responding, Asaya rested her head on his bare chest and fell back asleep. J lay there all night, running his fingers through her hair and trying to push the images of Rey fucking and touching his wife out of his head.

The next week went as usual. James would drop Asaya off at work and come back to take her to lunch, usually bearing gifts. He was still as sweet and romantic, but something was off. He seemed distant and she noticed that he had started to avoid Rey's calls. She was sure he did not know about her tryst with his friend, but could not figure out what was going on with those two. Asaya did not want to press him, because she knew his family had just buried William and he was upset about it. She had waited until she got some time away from James midweek while he was spending time with Will's parents and went through her bags from the getaway, disposing of anything that gave any clue about her misstep. It had been a rough week for her man and she just wanted to be there to support him any way she could. Asaya was relieved that Rey had stopped calling and stopped dropping by. Today, some of the Johnson family had come into town for the weekend and they were going to hang out at Mrs. Johnson's house, watching Friday night boxing and kicking it. They could use a little partying to relieve the stress. They got to Annette's house around ten o'clock that night and the gathering was already in full swing. They were greeted at the door by her brothers and some cousins Asaya had not seen in years. Mrs. Johnson grabbed her grandbaby and took him to her room to lay down with the other small children. He was tired and fell to sleep almost immediately. The adults had a good time watching the fight, playing dominoes, spades, ranking on one another and of course, drinking. James held off on drinking because he wanted to keep a clear head. Everyone was preparing to leave, when there was a loud knock on the door. It was after midnight and Asaya wondered who would be coming through this late.

One of the visiting cousins answered the door, then turned around and shouted, "James, there's some chick at the door for you." This immediately got everyone's attention and Asaya followed her man to the door to see whom the mystery woman was.

Before they got to the door, Tanya stepped inside, doing her best to look shy and intimidated. James was confused and asked, "What the fuck are you doing here, Tanya?" He could not believe the audacity of this bitch to show up at his mother-in-law's house after what she had done. He reached out to grab her and planned to throttle her, but his brothers-in-law held him back, telling him it was not worth it.

Asaya stepped to Tanya asking her who she was and why she was at her mother's house.

Tanya narrowed her eyes, dug in her purse, and pulled out the sandwich bag containing the positive pregnancy test. "Well, up until a couple of weeks ago, I was his woman," she snapped, pointing directly at James. She continued, "This is my pregnancy test. Congratulations, boo! You're going to be a daddy!"

Everyone swung around to look at James for an explanation, but he was speechless. Tanya turned around and walked back out the front door, disappearing into the night. Asaya slowly sat down, staring at the wall while fighting back tears. James looked at her as if he needed to say something, but no words would come.

BYE, BYE BABY

James stopped in front of the house and looked at Asaya pleadingly. He just wanted her to say something, but she had not spoken a word since they left her mother's house. JJ was already asleep, so Mrs. Johnson told them to leave him there for the night. They walked into the foyer of the home they shared and all hell broke loose. "So you bare-backing bitches?" she screamed so loud, he thought she had busted his eardrum. Before he could deny the accusation she was on him; punching him, scratching his face and crying. "I knew you were a fucking dog! I'm glad I didn't sleep with yo' dirty ass!" she yelled.

Unable to hold back any longer, James blurted out, "Oh, I'm the muthafuckin' dog? You clean, right, Asaya?" She stood there dumbfounded as to what he was getting at. "Do not play stupid, bitch!" he spat. "I found all the shit from Rey in the closet! You fuck my friend, you dirty ass hoe?" He waited for her response, but all Asaya could do was stand there. James was in a fit of rage and he was yelling in her face so close, she could feel his spit landing on her. He was calling her every name in the book as he backed her into a corner. J was so irate; tears began to run down his face. Asaya could not remember ever seeing him cry. All of a sudden, he brought his hand down and smacked the shit out of her. Asaya's head bounced off the wall and she crumpled to the floor. The hard thud of her head against the wall seemed to bring James back to his senses. He kneeled down next to her apologizing repeatedly, and trying to move her arm that was covering her face to assess the damage he had done. When he finally got her to show him her face, her left eye was damn near swollen shut and blood trickled from her nose and lip. He picked her up from the floor and led her to the bathroom. As she sat on the lid of the toilet, he wet a washcloth and attempted to clean up her face. He tried to get her to understand that things just got out of hand.

Asaya decided she was done turning a blind eye. She looked at James and said, "I'm leaving… now." He stepped aside and she pushed past him and ran upstairs, grabbing a few of her belongings. As Asaya ran out the front door, jumped in her car and sped off, James stood on the front porch watching until her taillights disappeared.

Rey answered the phone, sounding half-asleep, "Hello?"

"Hi, Rey, it's me, Asaya," she responded timidly.

Rey sat up straight at the sound of her voice. "Hey, Saya.

"What's wrong, baby? What's going on?" he asked. Not wanting to explain what happened over the phone, she asked him if she could come over his place. "Of course you can. I'll text you the address." Ironically, in all the time she had been with J, Asaya had never stepped foot in Rey's house. Maybe she knew deep down it would be risqué to be alone with him. She put the address in her GPS and took the forty-five-minute trip to his spot. When Rey answered the door, he looked refreshed. Seeing her bruised face, he quickly pulled her inside and sat her on the couch, leaving her only to grab supplies to doctor her up. As he gently cleaned her cut lip, he followed by kissing her wound. The sensation that went through her brought back everything she felt in Hawaii. She went over the night's chain of events, not leaving out a detail. She let Rey know that James had found out about them and would likely be on a rampage. He did not seem that worried. He decided he wanted to push the nail in the coffin on Asaya's marriage, so he told her about what went down with No Holds Barred. He told her how James had slipped up and screwed Carissa in his office, and gave her just what she needed to jack the club. He explained his life savings were in that safe, and everything he needed to open For the People Food Market. He told her that Carissa had never been found and James said he could not pay him back. He left out what he knew about Will and Carissa's murders. He wanted her to hate

James, but was not sure he could trust her with all of the details, especially since she already played him to the left.

The seeds of hatred he planted had already begun to sprout. Asaya could not fathom how she had given so many years to a man like James. For now, she wanted to forget about it all and Rey helped her to do just that. After a stiff drink to wash away her pain temporarily, he carried her into his bedroom and undressed her, down to her bra and panties. The sight of her shapely ebony body made him want to be inside her again. But Rey knew it was important that he show empathy tonight, so he tucked her in and lay down next to her, holding her close and kissing her injuries.

Tanya walked back and forth, unable to sleep. The morning could not come soon enough. She could not believe she just walked up to J's mother-in-law's house and threw that shit on the ground. If it were not for Rey, she would never have had the guts to pull such a stunt. She had been pregnant a few times before, and every time she made the announcement, she would be threatened into getting the pregnancy terminated. But Rey had assured her this time would be different. He had told her yesterday that she needed to leave his house and he put her up in a room for a couple of days. Although he did not say it, she knew he was expecting some chick to come through. It was crushing to be pushed aside for someone else once again, but soon she would be with her man, and have the family she always wanted. She got a text from Rey just before daylight, saying, "It's good." That was the signal Tanya needed to move to the next stage of the plan. She slipped on her shoes, grabbed her Michael Kors bag and jumped in the car, headed toward James' place of residence.

J sat on the couch in complete silence. Word had already got back to him that Asaya ran straight to Rey after their blowout. No doubt, the word was put out there by Rey himself. Although he declined a drink at the party, he drowned his sorrows in Hennessy now. It hurt that his woman had betrayed him this way; it hurt that he killed his little cousin over Rey's strip club. He knew that Asaya was gone forever by the way she looked through him that night. He knew there was no way she was going to stay with him after he had gone and had a baby on her. *But fuck her,* he thought, *she was just waiting for a reason to run right into Rey's arms.* He guessed that they might have been fucking around the whole time he was with her. She was always on the phone with him and he was always showing up, just in time to play Rescue Ronnie. Yes, they had both played him for a fool. Asaya was his son's mother, so he could not bring himself to harm her, but he would not piss on her if she were on fire. Rey, on the other hand, would pay with his life for what he did to J's family.

Tanya pulled up in front of the house where she hoped to live in the very near future. The sun was starting to rise and she wondered what kind of welcome she would receive from James. Her hands shook and she pulled the mirror down and touched up her make-up before getting out of the car. She took her time approaching the front door and knocked lightly. She barely had time to take a deep breath before the front door flung open and J stood there looking at her through angry eyes. "What the fuck are you doing on my porch?" he grumbled as he moved toward her. Unable to recite the speech she had prepared, she opened her purse and held it out in front of him. Curious as to what was going on, J peeked inside. He could not tell how much money was there, but there were several stacks of hundred-dollar bills. The purse also contained what appeared to be all the jewels she had taken from his safe.

"I'm sorry," she cried. "I will make up for everything I messed up," she pleaded. James looked her over, deciding whether he should beat the brakes off her ass. She took a big chance coming over here, especially after last night. She brought back what she took from him and was ready and willing to do whatever it took to get his forgiveness. That was a lot more than he could say for Asaya. He had changed his life for her and at the first problem, she ran back to Rey. She had shown what she was about and it was time he started looking at other options. He reached out toward Tanya and she flinched, afraid he was going to punch her. Instead, he grabbed her arm and pulled her into the house.

Asaya woke up to a throbbing headache. Her left eye was swollen completely shut and her top lip was so big, it could almost touch her nose. She vaguely remembered Rey telling her he would return shortly, so she was alone in his bed. She got up and stumbled to the bathroom, still off kilter from the fight with James and the drinks with Rey. She looked at herself in the mirror and it brought back everything that had happened last night. Tears stained her face and she considered all that was lost. She and J had both made mistakes in recent times, but they had made up and it seemed that from here on out it would be smooth sailing. The humiliation of that woman showing up at her mother's house, in front of the whole family, was too much to bear. There was no way she would raise another woman's illegitimate baby with her husband. Asaya was aware that J was frivolous and careless with his schlong, but she always thought he was sensible enough to use protection.

Their son had been meticulously planned and it was unlike him to impregnate random chicks. Asaya wanted a little brother or sister for JJ and James had always said he was not ready for more kids, or did not want any more. "I guess I know a lot less about him than I think," she mumbled to herself. She thought about how foolish she had been to leave Rey hanging after they got back from Hawaii. He had treated her better than J ever had and had been a true friend and confidante. Last night she made it priority to apologize for the way she had treated him and promised it would never happen again. She thanked God that Rey was understanding. Asaya powered on her phone and saw that she had multiple text messages from her mother and brothers, asking if she was okay and requesting that she call and check in. She called her mother and Mrs. Johnson picked up the phone on the first ring, sounding like she was out of breath.

"Asaya, are you alright, baby?" she panted.

"I'm okay, Mom," she responded.

She was just noticing that her voice was muffled due to her swollen lips.

"You don't sound okay, baby. James came by this morning and got JJ. He said he had no idea where you were!" her mother exclaimed. After assuring her mother that she was okay, she told her she was with Rey and he was looking out for her. In the past, Mrs. Johnson always had a sense of relief when Rey was with her daughter, but this time she responded with silence.

"Mom? Are you still there?" Asaya asked.

"Yes, I'm here. Saya... James told us that you were in Hawaii with Rey and that you were messing with him. Is that true?" she inquired, hoping it was misinformation. Asaya sighed in disappointment. Now he was dragging her name through the mud to her relatives. Dodging the question, she told her mother she would call her later and hung up the phone. She called her job and let them know she had a family emergency and would be out for the day.

Lastly, she made the call she had been putting off all morning. She dialed James' number and it rang several times before he finally picked up. "Yeah." he greeted dryly.

"Hey, J. My mom said you picked up JJ this morning and I wanted to find out what the plan is for him," she said timidly.

James seemed to have it all planned out. "You can pick him up tonight at eight o'clock if you want. From there, I say we switch every couple of days. I also have your things packed for you, so you can pick them up tonight, too."

Asaya could not believe how mechanical it all was with

J. He had gone from swooning over her just yesterday, to dismissing her from his life. With nothing else to say, she agreed to his terms and hung up.

A few minutes after she got off the phone, Rey came bounding through the door with fresh flowers and breakfast. Asaya stared at him blankly. He was acting as if he was on cloud nine, and her life had just been turned upside down. She thanked him for the flowers and went to the kitchen to locate a vase for them. As she was filling it, Rey appeared behind her, kissing her neck. She was not in the mood, but did not push him away. Asaya sat the vase full of flowers on the counter and Rey spun her around to face him. Unexpectedly, he dropped to one knee and produced a small red velvet box from his pocket. Asaya only had one good eye, but that was more than enough to see that he was about to propose to her. "Asaya Johnson," he started, "will you marry me?"

She ran his words back in her head, thinking, *Wait! did he just call me by my maiden name as if I'm not already married?* "Rey, you know I'm still married to James—" she replied, baffled by this awkward moment.

"I know… but not for long…" He stood up and turned around, grabbing some paperwork off the counter behind him. "I met with my attorney on your behalf and had him draw up this paperwork. It's all filled out. You just need to sign it, baby. You can end that shit and we'll be together forever," he said proudly.

Asaya backed up and gave him a puzzled look. "Don't you think things are going a little fast, Rey?" she asked.

"No. I have wanted to be with you forever. In my opinion, it ain't going fast enough," he replied and awaited her response.

Asaya took the ring and the paperwork from him, answering irritably, "Let me hold on to these while I digest everything that's happening. I didn't envision a marriage proposal with my eye fucked up." She stormed out of the kitchen and back to the room to rest on the bed.

Rey was not even slightly regretful about pushing her to make a decision. He felt he had been more than patient. He was taking no chances this time. He knew how much Asaya valued her wedding vows, so if he could get her to divorce James and marry him, he would surely have her allegiance and commitment as long as they lived.

As Asaya pulled up in front of the house that she had lived in for the last five years, she called James and let him know she was outside, per his request. She guessed he wanted to show her that she was no longer welcome in the home. His name was the only one on the mortgage, so until she filed for divorce and went to court, she was officially homeless. James made tenfold what she did for income, but since his was from hustling, it would be hard to prove, and a court would likely end up charging her alimony and child support. She would have to start looking for a new place.

James came outside holding Little J, who was excited to see his mommy. The innocent boy was oblivious to all the chaos going on around him, but he immediately asked his mommy what was wrong when he saw her face. J leaned into the passenger side window to find out what his son was referring to and Asaya thought for a moment that he was going to start apologizing again.

Before he could utter a word, the woman that had shown up at Mrs. Johnson's house came walking out in a robe, carrying Asaya's luggage. James thought it would feel good to have Tanya throw the situation in his wife's face, but he could not help wishing he had not done it. Tanya dropped the bags on the curb, gave Asaya a smirk and walked back inside. James walked around the bags, opened the back door and strapped JJ into the car seat, careful to avoid eye contact with Asaya. He then stepped back around the suitcases and followed Tanya into the house, closing the door behind him. Asaya sat there for a moment, trying to keep her tears at bay, before lugging the bags into the trunk and driving off. She needed to find a temporary resting place for the night. She was too embarrassed to face her family right now and she certainly did not want her brothers to see what J had done to her. Things would be completely out of her control then.

Rey had wanted to come with her to pick up JJ but she declined the offer, not wanting to add fuel to the fire. He was pressuring her to stay at his apartment, but she did not feel comfortable bringing her baby around a new man this soon. Rey was quick to point out that he was not a new man; but the dynamics of his and Asaya's relationship had changed. He had been calling Asaya all evening since the time she said she had to pick up her son. He was starting to worry that she had once again returned to James. If that were the case, there would not be a third chance for her. He drove past Mrs. Johnson's house and didn't see the gold Nissan Altima parked outside, so he called to see if she had seen her daughter. Annette simply replied "No," and hung up on him. Rey was not used to her being so rude, so he figured she had gotten wind of what went down. He cruised by James' house next and was relieved to find that Asaya was not there either. Just as he was leaving the neighborhood, she called. "Hi Rey, what you up to?" she asked.

"Just out and about taking care of business," he lied. She

let him know that she and JJ had posted up in a hotel near the airport for the next few days.

He expressed his discouragement that she had not taken him up on his offer to stay at his place. It was not like he was a stranger. He was around her son more than anyone was, outside of his parents. Rey pretended to understand her decision and drove home to spend the evening alone.

PUTTING IT ALL TOGETHER

It had been several weeks since everything went down at Mrs. Johnson's house and Asaya had come to terms with the fact that life as Mrs. Buchanan was over. She had gotten her own apartment, which Rey insisted that he furnish for her, so she let him. He was still upset that she had not filed the divorce papers he got for her. But at least, she had taken off James' wedding ring in exchange for the three-carat princess cut diamond he gave her. When Asaya's son was with her, she stayed at her own place, but let Rey tag along when she took him out for recreation.

When JJ was with his dad, Asaya stayed at Rey's place. It was not exactly what he had in mind, but at least they were beginning to feel like a real family. They kept it low key because she wanted to avoid any run-ins with James. The situation with him and Rey was so volatile that she would not be surprised if they killed one another. Today, they would head to South Seattle for Rey's annual family barbecue at Seward Park. Asaya had always been close with his people and was looking forward to seeing them.

James pulled up in front of his new establishment. Today would be the grand opening and he was hoping all would go as planned. Tanya rubbed his head gently, reassuring him that everything would be fine. He had not fallen in love with her, but she was down for him and he was really starting to like having her around. She was working hard on replacing the things that Asaya had brought to the household, and he knew she would never pull any foul shit on him again. He had not planned on having a baby with her, but now that she was pregnant and Rey was with his soon-to-be-ex-wife, he figured he would rather have his seed with him than not. He did not completely trust Tanya, though. One of the many conditions he set for letting her be with him was that she get a DNA test immediately after the baby was born. He was sure he had strapped up every single time, but because he was under the influence a lot back then, there was room for error. She agreed and he decided to give it a chance. He made sure he only let Tanya in on select information. He did not tell her a thing about Rey's betrayal. He did not need some chick in the streets running back pillow talk to everyone. The first week after Asaya left, he found himself in a downward spiral, picking up old habits and impeding his own progress. He had regained control and came up with a genius plan to start the process of making his childhood friend suffer, while boosting his own net worth. He and Tanya exited the car and he greeted his new employees as he walked into his business. He smiled to himself as he waved to the crowd of bustling customers waiting for the doors to open. Tanya looped her hand tight around his arm, feeling special for the first time in her life. She smiled because she was actually by the side of a successful businessman. As James stopped in front of the cash registers, all of the employees gathered around. His manager handed him an oversized pair of scissors and he walked over to the front entry, where he cut the red ribbon. Everyone cheered and the customers rushed in to be the first people to shop in the new store. James needed to go check on his indoor garden next, but dared not take Tanya with him. She would stay at the store making sure things ran well in his absence, and he would pick her up in a couple of hours.

Rey pulled up in front of Asaya's apartment and she walked out with Little J, holding his hand. He licked his lips as he checked her out. She was wearing a pair of fitted shorts that were almost Daisy Dukes, but not as vulgar; Rey thought she looked sexy, but completely appropriate for a family function. The pair of wedges and colorful sleeveless blouse he had bought her went perfectly with her shorts. As usual, Asaya had coordinated her son's blue short outfit to match her attire. He loved how meticulous she was about her and her little man's appearance. After securing JJ in the back, she sat on the passenger seat and waited for Rey to shut the door for her. As they pulled off, he and his lady held hands. He felt like everything was finally going his way. Rey decided to roll through his old hood on the way to Seward Park, and he and Asaya were chatting and enjoying each other's company as they rode down Rainier Avenue. Without warning, Rey slammed on the brakes and Asaya had to place her palm on the dashboard to brace herself. She turned around and checked to make sure her son was okay. She turned to face Rey and asked angrily, "What the fuck? Little J could have been hurt!"

He did not respond, so she followed his glaring eyes to what was supposed to be the new location of the Silver Spoon restaurant. The parking lot was packed and Rey parked in a handicapped spot, too impatient to circle around looking for anything else. As Asaya stood up out the car, she looked up at the sign that read, "For the People Food Market". Her jaw just about dropped to the ground at the realization of what happened. James had stolen Rey's dream! She took JJ out of the car and rushed in behind her irate man, trying to calm him down before it was too late. He was snatching up employee after employee, demanding to know where J was. She stood back, afraid to get in his way as he stalked over to the customer service counter. She stood behind him as he berated the manager and told him he was not leaving until the owner showed up. Powerless to do anything, Asaya just held her baby tight and waited for the scene to unfold.

Tanya walked out of the bathroom in the back of the store, drying her hands. She glanced over at the customer service counter and immediately recognized her friend, Rey. They had not talked since she moved back in with James and she wanted to thank him for making it happen. As she approached, she stared at the woman and child standing behind him in line. "That's Little J and his mom," she whispered to herself.

She watched as Asaya rubbed Rey's arm, prodding him to calm down and saying, "Baby, come on."

Tanya stopped dead in her tracks and backed up to hide behind a shelf. She saw the couple finally give up and leave the store. She was so upset; her hands would not stop shaking. She could not believe that Rey used her as a pawn to get his boy's woman. She realized that he had ruined her relationship and the trust she had established with James, all so he could get Asaya to leave with him. Tanya ran into the bathroom to pull herself together and wash her face. She was tired of people pretending they cared about her, only to have them use her. She was in a good position and the only person she owed anything was her man. Rey tried to play her like everyone else. She thought he was different, but now knew he was never a friend. She walked back out of the restroom, smiling and complimenting every worker she passed on a job well done.

Asaya sat silently in the car next to Rey. She had no idea what to say or do to make him feel better. For the People had been in the makings since childhood, and by taking it from him, James had just raised the stakes in this beef. Rey cursed himself for making the mistake of disclosing his goals to his former friend. He had even left his business plan in J's car a while back. Not foreseeing how big a deal it would become; he asked his boy to store it for safekeeping and had never gotten around to retrieving it. He gripped the steering wheel tightly, frustrated at himself for not getting his shit back. He had given J the blueprint to take what meant the most to him. Rey decided it was time to stop playing games and start treating James Buchanan like the enemy he had become. He did his best to put the situation in the back of his head and focus on the reunion they were headed to. Asaya kept touching his hand and looking at him sympathetically. They had spent countless nights with him telling her what he was going to do with the supermarket and how he would help his community. If there was one person in this world that knew the gravity of what just happened, it was she. He gently squeezed her hand, inaudibly signaling that he was good and they would still enjoy the day.

James got the urgent call from Tanya and she filled him in on the visit to the store from Rey. J expected him to catch wind of what he had done eventually, but things were moving a lot faster than anticipated. He knew Rey would be out for blood and so would he. He reached into the center console and checked his gun to make sure it was loaded and ready. He circled the block a few times to make sure Rey was not lurking in the area and awaiting his arrival. After gathering some clothing and personal effects, he decided they would get a room for the night and lay low to let the initial backlash blow over. He knew Rey would not do anything public like burn down the store or engage in a shootout. He would kick in a back door if he could get away with it. James had expected Asaya to call him, asking how he could have done such a thing, but she never did. As he and Tanya settled in the room at the DoubleTree for the night, she sat next to him on the bed and insisted that they talk. She immediately blurted out, "Rey set you up." J propped himself up on his elbows and leaned back, waiting for her to go into detail. "I was trying to get at him and he kept turning me down… He finally acted like he was interested, but only to offer me some money to get at you. He paid me every time I hooked up with you at the room and everything. After you kicked me out, he told me to take your money from the safe and let me stay at his place until he got back in town. I told him I wanted to give it back and be with you. He sent me to your girl's momma's house, and he told me to come over the morning I showed back up… he was sure you would take me back." James sat there, unable to believe his boy would do this to him. He could not grasp why he would go to these lengths.

Then Tanya added something that made it all come together. She lowered her head and said, "I thought he was helping me because we were friends… until I saw him with your wife and son today. He used me to get her to leave you." He sat there interpreting the chain of events and contemplating how he would react.

He looked at her and replied, "I appreciate your honesty, T. This may not end the way you want it to, but you are a good person and I will always respect you and be a friend." He meant them to be words of comfort, but all she heard was that he did not love her, and that she could be nothing more than a friend. Then again, she had already known that.

She was tired of lying and trying to sleep her way to the

top, so she decided to go a step further with her confession. "I'm-I'm not pregnant by you, J. I thought I was at first. When I went to the doctor and they told me how far along I was, I realized it couldn't be you. I wanted to tell you before, but—"

James put his hand up, indicating that he wanted her to stop talking. She scooted back in case he lashed out, but James was not angry with her. In fact, he was relieved. He was having a hard time coming to terms with the fact that he was having a baby with a woman he had no feelings for, so this was welcome news. She told him that she thought it was her ex-boyfriend's baby and she wanted to tell him and see if they could reconcile. This dramatic lifestyle was okay for Tanya, but she wanted her child to have a chance at a normal life. She recalled how poorly she had treated Steven, and hoped he would forgive her and want to be a father. Now that he knew he had not procreated with another woman while he was married, he was even more upset about Asaya's betrayal. He was conflicted because he knew she was just as in the dark as he was and in spite of her actions, he still loved his wife and wanted her back. He assured Tanya that her loyalty would be reciprocated and he would make sure she was taken care of. He also promised to do whatever he could to help her reunite with Steven.

The two hugged briefly and each settled into their own beds for a good night's rest. Tanya put her phone on silent mode and didn't notice the screen lighting up repeatedly as Rey tried frantically to reach her.

Rey lay across his bed silently staring at the ceiling. He had been trying to reach Tanya ever since dropping Asaya and Little J off at home. He needed to get the inside track on the security system at J's spot. He had watched the house all night, but saw no one coming or going. They had to return sooner or later, and it was only a matter of time before James had to face Rey. He knew that ever since Tanya jacked him, J had invested in the best residential security system possible and it would be hard to get into his house without having a confrontation with either the police, or J himself. This would have to be done the right way. Rey had not really spoken to Tanya since she was back in the house with J. She had sent a text message on a couple of occasions, asking how he was doing. He was preoccupied with Asaya, so he had kept his responses short and had not really inquired about what was going on with her. He regretted that now. He had noticed that Tanya's needy ass was susceptible to any man that showed her any type of attention, so he knew that James likely had the upper hand and her devotion. The fact that she did not even attempt to reach him with a warning about what James was doing with the store let him know that her allegiance had changed. He had looked out for her over the past couple of months and if there was one thing Rey did not respect, it was a traitor. He sat up and downed his drink on the table next to the bed to help ease his mind enough to sleep. Rey was jarred awake early the next morning by Tanya finally returning his call. She had a little bit of time to herself while J was out getting them breakfast. "What's going on, Tanya?" he demanded upon picking up.

"Not much… you called?" she responded dryly.

"So you helped J fuck me over?" he questioned.

"I didn't help nobody do nothing. I had no idea anything was going on, Rey," she explained.

"Well I need you to meet me so I can get some info from

you, T," he ordered.

"Look, Rey, I know why you sent me after J. I saw you

with his wife and kid. You dirty," she chided.

"So what you tryin' to say?" he asked.

Tanya replied confidently, "I ain't your slave and I won't

be doing any more of your dirty work. I told him everything

about us and I'm not in your crazy plan to obsess over this chick. So we're done!"

Rey couldn't believe she had the nerve to speak with him like this. Before he could respond, she had hung up on him. Now that J knew that Rey had sent Tanya to seduce him and that he was not having a kid with her, he would no doubt be out to get Asaya back at any cost. Rey would need to keep his lady as close to him as possible and as far away from James as he could. He needed insurance to make sure he did not slip up and lose another woman to his rival. He called Asaya and asked her if they could meet for brunch and she turned him down, because she needed to be at church. With everything going on, she had not been in a couple of weeks and she could use some words of wisdom and prayer right now. She told Rey she would meet him after church for a late lunch.

Asaya sat in the back pew at Christ the King, hoping to avoid the eyes of the elders in the church. Every time she missed a service or two, they would keep glancing at her throughout the sermon to let her know she was guilty. After making sure she drew no attention, she carefully removed her sunglasses and sat back to enjoy the sermon. She did not bring Little J with her this time, because it was James' day to be with him. She had dropped him off at her mother's house before church and James was to pick him up later on. Asaya felt like someone was watching her and nearly ran out of the church when she saw James sitting a couple of pews ahead of her, intensely looking back. Her heart felt like it would pound out of her chest. She recounted how angry he had gotten the night she found out about his baby. They had gotten into scuffles in the past and he had pushed her, but never had he hit her. She looked down to escape his gaze, not wanting to provoke him. She pulled out her phone and was going to call Rey, but her hands were trembling so badly she could not dial. She looked up to find that J had turned around to face the front. She noticed Little J happily clapping on his lap. Then she saw *her*. Tanya was sitting in the pew behind James and JJ. Asaya quickly transitioned from scared to death, to mad as hell. She wanted to go slap the shit out of both of them, but her legs would not move. So she sat there anxiously waiting for service to end. She could not believe he would do this; he brought his jump off to her church. Everyone here knew Asaya and she was still recovering from the last time he humiliated her. When the service ended, she exited the double doors and almost ran to her car. As she went across the parking lot, she could hear James calling her name.

"Asaya, come here!" he yelled. She tried to get to her car,

get in and lock the doors, but he had already beat her there and cut off her escape route.

"What do you want, James?" she asked, keeping space between them.

"I need to holla at you," he said.

"We have nothing to talk about. Why don't you go get our son from that chick and leave me alone?" she cried. When Tanya asked to go to church with him that morning, he readily agreed because he knew she needed it. It never occurred to him that his wife would be there, or what it may look like to everyone there. He reached out to pull Asaya close to him; she jumped back like he had stung her.

"Look Saya, I am sorry about everything, baby. This ain't what it looks like. Rey set me up and she ain't having my baby," he reasoned.

"Wow! You always sorry…. you find a way to blame everything you do on someone else! Rey has been a better man to me than you ever have! Now get out my way!" No longer afraid of him, she brushed past him, got in the car and sped away. James tried to stop her to no avail.

"Damn!" he muttered as he walked back toward the church.

Asaya pulled into the Olive Garden to meet Rey for lunch. She had decided he was dealing with enough issues, so she would not add to them by telling him about the episode at Christ the King. She pulled down the mirror on the visor to make sure her eyes were not puffy. Before she could get out of the car, Rey appeared and opened her door. He greeted her with a huge bouquet of long-stemmed pink roses and a small square box with a pink bow around it. "Oh, baby," she murmured, "You shouldn't be getting me gifts right now." Asaya could not believe he had taken the time to think about her when he was going through so much. She sat the flowers on the passenger seat and Rey escorted her into the restaurant. After they were seated, he asked her to open the gift. She gently removed the bow and slid the blue velvet box out. When she opened it, she immediately recognized the items inside; it was Rey's grandmother's wedding gift from his grandfather. His grandmother loved emeralds and the necklace and earrings had plenty of them, surrounded by sparkling diamonds. She had left them to Rey when she passed, wanting him to gift them to his wife someday. He had always kept them in a safe deposit box for security, but had shown them to his best friend when they were in college. Asaya was speechless. She did not necessarily feel like she had earned such a priceless gift yet. "I don't know what to say... Thank you, Rey," she reciprocated. She walked to his side of the table and leaned over to hug him. He pulled her down on his lap and kissed her like they were in a private setting, embarrassed by the public display of affection, Asaya pried his hands away and gave him one last peck before returning to her seat. They had light conversation over lunch and she was surprised to find him in an extremely upbeat mood. They were waiting for the bill when Rey's mood turned serious.

"Saya, I have to tell you some things," he said. Nervous about what was about to come, she braced herself for bad news. "We been close forever and there are some things I have been keeping from you. Now that we are together, I do not want any secrets between us," he said. Asaya listened as he proceeded to tell her about every way James had wronged her that he was aware of. He missed nothing; from the time that he spent Valentine's Day with her former best friend, to her old co-worker dating him behind her back. Most of what he told her, she already knew and she was not really surprised by the rest. She was turned off by Rey though. He had never been the type to throw salt on the next man, but for some reason, he was doing it today. She had always respected him for standing on his own merits, but now he felt like he had to shorten J's straw to keep Asaya. It made him look desperate. She thanked him for his honesty and they left the restaurant.

James sat in the car with his son, waiting on Tanya to come out of the coffee shop. When she called Steven and told him that she was having his child, he did not believe her. James had called him back and confirmed what Tanya said, apologizing to the other man for snaking him for his girl. Reluctantly, Steven agreed to meet up with her and go over how they could either co- parent the little one successfully or raise the baby together. J had messed around with many women that were in relationships before. Some of them were even married. This was the first time he actually regretted doing it. Steven seemed like a good guy and he would have definitely loved Tanya and treated her better than J would have. He hoped everything would work out for them. About thirty minutes after arriving, Tanya came walking out with a smile on her face. James could tell the meeting must have gone well by her body language. He was eager to find out what the outcome was. As she approached the car, he leaned over and opened the passenger door for her. Two shots rang out, shattering the peaceful sunny day. J immediately squeezed between the seats and pulled his son's head down covering him. When he was sure there would be no more gunfire, he sat up with his own pistol cocked and ready. The scene outside was chaotic as people ran for cover and checked each other for injuries. On the ground outside the car, Tanya laid on her back. A puddle of blood had formed near her head and her hazel contacts stared up at the sunny sky. J looked down at her one last time. "Damn, T..." he lamented as he reluctantly closed the door and pulled away. He looked in his rearview mirror just in time to see Steven sitting on the ground with Tanya in his arms.

Rey hung up the phone and powered it off.

"Who was that?" Asaya asked in a groggy tone.

"Sounded like a prank call," he lied. He returned to his spooning position with his lady and was immediately aroused by the feeling of her naked body pressed firmly against his. He began kissing the back of her neck and in no time, she was as hot and bothered as he was and ready for round two. After he stroked her back to sleep, he laid awake with Asaya in his arms while plotting his next move. When he saw James at Christ the King trying his best to convince Saya that he had been set up, he knew that although she did not believe him, once Tanya was able to back up his story that may have changed. Now that he knew the opportunistic hood rat was out of the equation, no one could co-sign for J. He would still need to find a way to get rid of him for good, and get back For the People.

J entered the code to arm the security system. He placed his gun on top of the shelf in the corner of the living room. He would have kept it on him, but with Little J in the house, he did not want to take any chances. The image of Tanya lying on the ground with her brains blown out kept circulating in his mind. He could not help but wonder what else he could have done to save her. He did not get a look at the shooter, but had no doubt that it was Rey's doing. It looked like he would stop at nothing to keep Asaya, including murder. James wished he knew more about Tanya, so he could reach out to her family and offer his condolences. But the reality of the situation was that no matter how bad he felt about what happened, he could never be connected to her or her killing. He could not be the subject of a police investigation when some of his business ventures were not necessarily on the up and up. He had only communicated with Steven from Tanya's phone and she left it in the car when she went into the coffee shop. After leaving the scene, James removed that battery and drove to Lake Washington where he disposed of it. One thing was for sure; he would not send his son anywhere near Asaya as long as she was around Rey, and he would find a way to save her before it was too late. He pulled his baby boy close to him and held him tight as he slept, vowing to never let anything happen to him.

VENGEANCE

Asaya slid out of bed and retrieved her nightie off the floor, pulling it over her head. Rey had to do some work this morning, so he had left early and would not be returning until this afternoon. She called the office to let them know she would be out once again today. Lately, Asaya was using all of the vacation time she had saved up over the past few years. She grabbed her phone off the bedside table. She went to power it up, but it was already on. "That's funny... I could've sworn I turned this off," she mumbled to herself. She brushed the thought aside, knowing she had a few drinks yesterday evening and could not be sure. She scrolled through the call log and found not a single call from James. She expected several calls and messages after the scene he made after church. Just like on cue, the phone rang and "The Other Half" showed up on the screen. She answered, trying not to sound too excited to hear from him. Before she could say anything, James started talking.

"Saya, you have to get away from Rey," he said.

"Here you go again. Is this what you called f—"

He cut her off saying, "He killed Tanya yesterday."

Finding what J was saying hard to believe, she decided

to hear him out. "Look, J. I know a lot has happened and I really am sorry something happened to your girl, but Rey did not do it. He was here with me all day and night." She stopped speaking, aware of the implications surrounding her last statement. Unable to convince her that Rey was anything but Prince Charming, J gave up and just asked her to be careful and to keep his son away from him. She agreed to do so for now and hung up. She really felt sorry for the young lady that was shot and killed. She did not know what she was caught up in, but Asaya figured it must have been something serious. It seemed that J was starting to get obsessive about hating Rey. Asaya hoped he would come to his senses before something horrible happened. She showered and got dressed to go pick up some fresh clothing from her place.

As soon as she got to the door, Asaya knew something was very wrong. The wood near the doorknob was splintered and the front door was open a couple of inches. She reached in her purse and pulled out her .22 caliber pistol. Cautiously pushing the door open, she stepped inside. The first thing she saw was her new living room set completely destroyed. The burgundy leather was shredded and covered with splashes of black paint. Her coffee table and end tables were all smashed to smithereens. Along the wall behind the couch, the word "WHORE" was written in black paint. Asaya made her way through the rest of the apartment and was relieved to find that whoever caused this destruction was long gone. The vandalism throughout the apartment was just as devastating as it was in the living room. All of the new dishes and appliances in the kitchen were smashed on the floor. Food from the refrigerator was scattered throughout the apartment. In the bedroom, the mattress was covered with what smelled like piss, and all of Asaya's clothing ripped up and thrown everywhere. She looked at the dresser and ran over to her jewelry box. Opening it, the only items missing were a couple of costume pieces and the wedding ring J had given her. She had stopped wearing it weeks ago and replaced it with the engagement ring from Rey. Whoever broke in certainly did not intend to rob the place. They had destroyed anything of value or simply left it, with the exception of the ring. She rushed into her son's room to find that it was the only place that was spared from someone's fit of rage. "James!" she uttered in disbelief. It only made sense. He messed up everything Rey had given her, took his ring and left JJ's stuff alone. To her, this meant that he was a lot more dangerous than she thought; one minute he was professing his love and the next, kicking her door in. Asaya gathered the few pieces of clothing that were usable and ran to her car. She thought about calling the police, but knew she could not prove J's guilt. He was already acting like he had lost his damn mind and it was likely that contact from the police would only push him further over the edge. She dialed Rey in a panic, hoping he was nearby.

"Hey, what up, baby?" he answered in his strange cheerful mood.

"James kicked in my door and destroyed my apartment, Rey!" she exclaimed.

"Are you there right now... is *he* there right now?" he asked anxiously.

"No, he is not here. I'm sitting in front," she answered.

"Stay there. I'm right up the street. Gimme ten minutes, Saya," he said empathetically. She sat in her car, unable to hold back the tears that streamed down her face. It made no sense that he was out to get her because she finally got sick of his shit and left. *If anyone should be out for blood, it should be me,* she thought. Rey pulled up next to her and she got out and greeted him. Aware that she had been crying, he wrapped his arms tightly around her and held her for several minutes before leading her back up to the apartment, so he could survey the damage. After looking over the place, he told her not to worry; he would have everything back in order within a week and would even get a security system for protection. Asaya thanked him for the offer, but told him she no longer wanted to reside there. Now that J had shown himself to be off his rocker, she would not be a sitting duck when he returned. She needed to lay low and make sure he never found out where she was staying. "You can stay with me, baby," Rey offered. "I got plenty of space and we can move JJ's stuff to my guest bedroom. I want to make sure y'all are safe," he continued. Asaya happily agreed, thankful that Rey was here for her. He got on his phone and made a few calls, setting up the move and repairs before telling her to follow him back to his place. As soon as they drove off, Asaya called James.

As soon as he picked up, she started going off. "You punk ass little boy! Why would you tear up my house?"

James acted confused as to what she was referring to. "What? I have no idea what you are talking about!" he yelled. Exasperated with his denial, Asaya disconnected the call.

James sat on top of the hill at the graveyard. He used his binoculars to watch Tanya's family and friends pay their last respects to her. He never knew she had such a big family. The whole time they were acquainted, she talked about being alone and an outcast, but from their strong features, he could tell that she had several siblings and even a mother and father that were both alive and well. He expected to find one lone visitor mourning her loss, but there was no shortage of people that cared about T. Steven was there, sitting motionless in the front row with dark glasses on. J could not tell if he was crying or not from so far away, but everyone that walked by seemed to stop and comfort him. Among the flowers on top of her casket were the roses J had sent anonymously. He also spotted the funeral wreaths he sent nearby. First Rey played him and got him to have his own flesh and blood killed, and now he had murdered an innocent bystander caught in the middle of this feud. She had no business losing her life over this, but Rey was the one that dragged her into it and he was the one that eventually took her out. Had J been walking with her out of the coffee shop that day, he was certain; there would be two funerals in progress today.

This war was about to come to an end one way or another. A few years back when Rey was still in the game, he had gotten caught up in a turf war with a d-boy named K.D. from the Central District and he refused to back down. Rey ended up running into him on the solo and had to take K.D.'s life in order to save his own. The first place he ran was to J's house, covered in blood from head to toe and with the body still in his trunk, alongside a bloody hammer. Both men knew that if it got out that Rey was responsible for the killing, many more from both the South End and the Central District would meet the same fate. No one would be safe, including their parents, grandparents and children. James helped him to dispose of the body and clean up the mess, and even set him up with an alibi. Everyone was aware of the beef and Rey would be the first person they looked to for answers. In the end, with no body, no evidence and an airtight alibi, there was not enough proof for the police to arrest anyone, or for the community or for K.D.'s homeboys to go to battle over it. But J had kept a trump card. He had seen it all too many times; one man commits a crime and he drags his closest friend into it to save his own skin. While Rey was busy panicking, J had put the murder weapon in an undisclosed location. He had also taken a picture of the deceased man in his homeboy's trunk and a flick of the blood-soaked clothing, including a shirt with R.L. stitched across it. Rey never questioned J about what he did with all of the items. He was sure that his tracks were covered and eventually, everyone all but forgot it happened, everyone except for James. He had meant to dispose of the items once and for all, but kept procrastinating. Now they were just what he needed to finish Rey. J sealed the box, careful not to let the tape stick to his rubber gloves. He used a black Sharpie to address the package to K.D.'s brother, Jason. Since James and Rey got out of the game and after the demise of his brother, J.D. had taken over his old territory and he was ruthless. No one stepped foot in his hood without authorization. He had been trying to find out what happened to his big bro for years and if he ever did, somebody would have hell to pay. J printed an express mailing label offline from a Kinko's about thirty miles south of Seattle before placing the package in a drop box. He wanted to be sure he was never connected to the delivery.

Asaya sat on the couch leaned back against Rey's chest while he gently stroked her hair. He leaned down and breathed in the odor of her freshly washed locks. He put his arm around her waist and squeezed her gently as he kissed her forehead. She looked up at him and smiled, feeling safe and secure in his arms. The faint sound of JJ snoring in his new bedroom could be heard every now and then over the television. Asaya was afraid he would have a hard time adjusting to his new environment, but he loved it and did not put up a fight at bedtime. Everything felt like it was just as it should be. It was as if Rey was meant to be her man and she and her son belonged here with him. All hell was going to break loose when James found out they were living here, but as long as she kept the location a secret and minimized her contact with him, she was not that worried about it. J had been calling her phone all day, leaving message after message, warning her to stay away from Rey and accusing him of killing people. She only responded once via text message, letting him know that his desperation was not a good look before finally blocking his calls. Everything was falling into place for Rey. He had his woman and her son here with him, so there was no reason for her to be in contact with her ex. Once her divorce was final, he would marry her immediately and they would have their own kids. She had never gotten around to signing the paperwork his lawyer drew up, so he had taken it upon himself to sign her name and file the paperwork for dissolution of marriage. Rey did not want the stigma of her being a widow overshadowing his marriage to Asaya. He knew what was best for his woman and in the end, she would thank him for looking out for her.

Mrs. Johnson looked concerned when her daughter showed up to drop JJ off for an overnight visit. They had not really talked since the evening Tanya showed up at the family get- together. "Hey baby," she started as she touched Asaya's shoulder, "I'm worried about you. Is everything okay?"

Asaya looked her mom directly in the eyes to let her know she was being honest. "Mommy, I am good. Everything has worked out and I am happy." She hugged Annette and smiled at her, before handing over Little J and driving off. Her mother watched as she turned around the corner and out of view. Regardless of what her daughter had said, she was still uneasy about all the drama going on and her grandson being caught in the middle. She had gone by Asaya's apartment and found it vacant yesterday. There was a crew there cleaning up paint, patching holes in the walls and moving broken furniture. Since it was not mentioned, she had not questioned her child about it, but assumed Asaya had shacked up with Rey. Mrs. Johnson loved Rey like one of her own, but she did not like the way he was doing things lately. He was James' friend and despite what was going on in the Buchanan marriage, you do not sleep with your best friend's wife. She had always appreciated the way Rey protected her daughter, but now she suspected he had ulterior motives all along. No... everything was not alright... not even close.

When Asaya got home, Rey had already left to handle his business affairs. She planned to unpack some of her belongings since she had left cardboard boxes throughout his meticulous living room. She put away what was left of her dishes and some food items she had retrieved from the cupboard of her apartment. The next box she opened contained a purple shoebox with pink polka dots on it. She recognized it as the place she kept all of the mementos she had collected over the years. She carried the box over to the coffee table and sat on the couch to go through it. Asaya's eyes got misty as she viewed the family pictures of her, James, and their baby. J looked so proud of his mini-me and Asaya looked like she was so in love. She tried to remember if she was really miserable, but smiling for the camera that day all she could recall was being head over heels for her new family. She wiped a tear that dropped onto the picture with her sleeve before placing it back in the box. She was about to put the lid on when she spotted a small taupe jewelry box in the corner.

Removing the box, she slowly opened the lid to find

the very first pair of diamond earrings J had gotten her. They were one karat each and shaped like raindrops. They sparkled up at her, catching the beam of sunshine coming through the slider. Without thinking it through, Asaya pulled one of them out the box and put it in her ear. She picked up the second one, wanting to see how the pair looked on her nowadays. Before she could get it in, the earring slipped from her grasp and hit the floor, disappearing under the couch. She bent over and ran her hand along the edge of the sofa, but felt nothing. Sighing deeply, Asaya dropped to her knees and bent over to look under the couch. The earring was near the front and she picked it up, placing it on the table. There were more items under there and she figured she might as well get everything. She pulled out a gold shiny object and once she sat up on the floor, she realized it was familiar. She would know this ring anywhere; James' grandfather had given it to him when he graduated high school. It was his most treasured heirloom. In fact, it was his only one. J would never part with this willingly. Asaya suddenly had an epiphany. The ring was kept in the safe at the house—the safe that Tanya stole it from. Saya searched her brain for an answer as to how it got here in Rey's apartment. She bent down again to retrieve the other item she had spotted.

When she pulled the last piece of misplaced property out into the light, there was no more denying what was going on. She stared down into the face of the woman that had claimed to be pregnant by her husband. "TANYA LYNNETTE FORD", the Washington State Driver's License read. Asaya could feel the color drain from her face. It dawned on her that Tanya had been in Rey's house after she had stolen the money and jewels. J had been telling the truth when he said Rey set him up. Asaya was more afraid than she had ever been in her entire life. Her mind raced. *What if J was telling the truth about Tanya's murder, too? Could Rey actually kill someone?* She got off the floor and put the treasures she had found in her purse. Dialing Rey's number, she tapped her foot impatiently waiting for him to answer. When he finally picked up, she gave him an upbeat greeting, "Hey Rey. How are you, babe?" she asked.

"I'm good, sweetie. How about you?" he responded.

"I'm not so good, baby… I miss you and I wanted to see if we could go to Olive Garden again this afternoon," she fabricated.

"You can have whatever you like, baby. I'm in the middle of some things, but I should be done no later than three. After that, I'm all yours." he grinned.

Asaya thanked him sweetly and hung up. Looking at

the screen, she noted she had roughly four hours to get what she needed, and get the fuck out of there. She looked under every piece of furniture in the living room, even checking the couch cushions; she climbed on the kitchen counter, looking through the cupboards. She even checked the storage unit on the balcony, but found nothing else. Finally, she made her way to the bedroom. One evening, Rey thought she was asleep and he had retrieved a key out of one of his jackets in the closet before closing the door behind him. She had not been able to see exactly what he was doing, but knew there was some inconspicuous place that he kept important things. To her, the fact that this place required a key meant there was something worth protecting. She went into the closet and observed the row of perfectly pressed jackets hanging up. She dug through the pockets of several of them before she finally found the key she was looking for. Asaya swiveled her head to look for a safe. She did not see anything, so she started moving the clothes and looking at the wall behind them. In the back of the closet, she found a small doorknob sticking out from the wall. Sticking the key in the lock, she turned it and pulled and a small square in the wall opened up. As she ducked and walked inside, she pulled the cord in the low ceiling, turning on the light. She was speechless to find pictures of herself and her family everywhere. There were pictures of her and James running together, at her mother's house, at church. Anything she had done with her husband after returning from Hawaii was documented right here. Rey had been watching her and had already known she had rekindled her marriage. He pretended to be in the dark the whole time. On a small desk in the corner, she found several manila folders with names on them. Most of the names she did not recognize, but there were a couple that rang some bells. She pulled a folder labeled "Will Buchanan" and flipped it open. She almost dropped it when the picture of Will's dead body with two bullet holes in his head fell out. Covering her mouth to keep from shrieking, she looked through the remainder of the folder. There was a full-page report from some investigator talking about how Will had orchestrated the robbery of No Holds Barred and list of various banks he held accounts in. Running back to the table, she thumbed through another folder entitled "Carissa" and found another gruesome photo of her mangled body lying on a street corner. There were pictures of her and Will kissing and apparently living together. Lying on the table in plain sight was a wrinkled obituary with a picture of Tanya on front. Everyone that had died recently was right here in the secret room of the man she had been living with—the man she thought she knew better than anyone else did. She felt sick to her stomach at the thought of snuggling up to a murderer every night. She neatly placed everything back where she found it and started to turn around and leave when she spotted a shoebox on the floor in a dark corner of the room. Afraid of what she might find, she stood back and kicked the lid off it. Sitting on top of everything inside was her wedding ring; the same one that came up missing when her apartment was robbed. She knelt down and pulled the box closer. Inside, she also found wedding photos of her and James, and even their marriage certificate. She grabbed her chest, stunned at how deranged Rey really was. All this time she thought he was protecting her from her crazy husband, but he was the one she needed to be saved from. She grabbed the shoebox and ran out of the small room, not bothering to close the door or remove the key from the lock. She started going back and forth to her car in the parking lot, loading the boxes she had never unpacked. After the most important items were in the vehicle, she got her purse, jumped in the car and rushed toward the parking lot exit. As she was about to exit the complex, Rey's car pulled in front of her and stopped. She slammed on the brakes to avoid crashing into him and he got out, rushing to the driver's side of her car. Asaya hit the lock button just before he tried the door handle and he began banging on the window. "Open the door, Saya!" he demanded.

"Get your car out of my way, Rey!" she yelled.

"Baby, what's wrong? Why you got boxes in your car?" he asked. Knowing what he was capable of, Asaya did not want to risk getting him more upset than he already was. She threw the car into reverse and punched the gas, causing Rey to jump back to avoid his foot being run over. She turned the wheel away from him and drove around his car and off the curb, speeding down the street. She checked her rearview mirror and saw Rey hop in his car to come after her. Trembling with fear, Asaya thought about calling the police, but knew they would never make it in time. She put the gas pedal to the floor and he did the same. In front of her red lights started to flash as the railroad crossing arms began to lower. From what she saw, she had better odds against a train than Reyhan Lucas. Keeping her foot firmly on the gas, she barely missed the barricade and the oncoming train as she barreled across the tracks to safety. Rey screeched to a halt, unable to get across in time. Although he had been stalled, Asaya kept on speeding, wanting to put as much distance as possible between her and the stalker.

After zigzagging down back streets and making sure she had lost Rey, she dialed James. He answered and she started talking fast, "J! Rey killed everybody... Will, Carissa, Tanya... He broke in my place!" James knew his ex-partner had smoked Tanya and more than likely broke into Asaya's place, but he was confused as to why she thought he had killed Will and Carissa. Not wanting to go over details on the phone, he asked her to meet him in Woodinville at his grow spot. Asaya was not far from there, so they agreed it was best he pick up Little J and Mrs. Johnson, too, since Rey knew where to find them. This was the first time J would tell anyone but his employees the whereabouts of his lucrative venture. Asaya hit the road, heading toward the warehouse. James stopped by his mother-in-law's house and ordered both her and his son into the car. Of course, Annette protested, so he had to motivate her by letting her know her baby girl was in trouble.

Asaya paced back and forth in the lobby of her husband's business and was relieved when he pulled up, carrying two familiar faces. She ran outside and hugged her mom and her baby tightly, emotional from all of the turmoil. Unsure of their safety, Mrs. Johnson rushed inside with her grandson. James walked up to his wife and she looked down at the ground, ashamed that she had a part in bringing this situation with Rey upon their family. Knowing that this was hardly all Asaya's fault, J pulled her close to him and held her. She buried her head in his chest and began to sob uncontrollably. He stood there holding her until she got control of her emotions. James lifted her face and looked into her eyes. "Look, baby… this ain't your fault. None of this would have happened if it was not for me fucking off." She started to interrupt him and he put his finger to her mouth, forbidding her to speak. "We are gonna be cool. I'm gonna take care of us. Nothing is going to happen to any of us. You hear me?" He waited for her response. Asaya nodded as she wrapped her hands around his waist. He leaned in and kissed her softly on the forehead and then on her lips and said, "I love you, Asaya Buchanan." They turned and walked into the warehouse, locking the door behind them. Mrs. Johnson sat in the back office with JJ while his parents talked about everything Asaya had found in the hidden room at Rey's.

She told J about the flicks and report she found with Will and Carissa. He was surprised to find that his boy had known about the whole heist all along. That meant he also knew J had them taken out and got the money so back, but never returned it to him. It was no wonder he had been vindictive. It was not like Rey to try so hard to snake a nigga just for some pussy. James wished he would have just given back the money and avoided the fallout. But it was too late to cry over spilled milk. He had already started the wheel to turning on the downfall of Rey Lucas, and it would not be long before that problem was solved. J told Asaya that they would have to skip town until he was able to iron things out with Rey. In spite of what she found in that closet, James knew his wife still had and would likely always have strong emotions when it came to Rey. There was no way he could tell her he was going to get rid of the man permanently, so he told her what she wanted to hear. After all the bullshit she had pulled lately, she would have to regain his trust before he opened up to her like he used to. J had not been staying at his house lately and had put it up for rent to generate income. Now, he would take his family on an extended vacation until this mess blew over. They let Asaya's mom in on some of the details to get her to understand the severity of the circumstances. She finally agreed and by the next morning, Asaya, James, Annette and JJ were on the road, headed to a resort in Eastern Washington.

Rey punched a gaping hole in his bedroom wall. He had waited all night for Asaya to reach out to him andapologize for going in his shit. He let her stay in his place, because he thought she was a woman he could trust. Now he was realizing that she was just an average, run-of-the-mill bitch. She had a man willing to take care of her and treat her right. He would have even taken care of her son, but she turned out to be just like the rest of the low-budget bitches he grew up with. She seemed to like getting mistreated. Even after she ran back to J the first time, he took her back with open arms and pretended it never happened. He would not give her another chance. He planned to get rid of J and now that she had chosen to ride with her husband, she could die with him. He thought about how stupid Asaya was. She had everything she needed to put him away forever, but she only took a raggedy shoebox with her precious little wedding ring and pictures in it. Rey had been by the Buchanan house, only to find some new residents moving in. In watching Mrs. Johnson's house, he found that she had not been home in days either. He suspected she was also in hiding, because she had no life other than babysitting for her daughter. But they could not dodge him forever. When Asaya and J resurfaced, they would both wish they never crossed Rey.

Asaya flipped the last two pancakes over; proud of the country breakfast she had made for her family. As she stoodover the stove, J walked up behind her and slipped his arms around her waist. She closed her eyes and leaned back into him, circling one arm around his neck. She turned her face toward his and he eagerly kissed her mouth. She dropped the spatula and spun around to face him, closing her eyes as she sensually stuck her tongue in and out of his mouth until his erection was so hard, it was uncomfortable against her stomach. Unable to stand the temptation, he picked her up and sat her on the counter, lifting up the t-shirt she was wearing. He slipped her panties off and dropped them to the floor as he dropped to his knees in front of her. He spread her legs apart and pulled her ass close to the edge of the counter. Asaya leaned back against the cabinets, panting in anticipation of what was to come. Refusing to take his eyes off her, James stroked her throbbing punany with his lips and tongue until she convulsed in orgasm. Turned on by her soft moans, he stood up and dropped his boxers to the floor. Grabbing her hips, he hungrily devoured her mouth as he forcefully pushed himself inside of her. Asaya let out a cry when he entered her and he stiffened even more. J had not been with his wife in months and he must have forgotten how good it was. She was so wet, warm and tight, he was only a couple of minutes in before he started to cum uncontrollably, digging his fingertips into the flesh of her thighs. She ran her fingernails up and down his back as he held on for dear life. When he finally stilled, they both stayed still for a while, not knowing how to react to what just happened between them. James lifted Asaya to the floor, but kept his arms around her. He struggled to find the right words to say. "Was it okay, baby?" she asked. Expecting one of his after-sex insults she was so familiar with, she braced herself.

"It was beyond okay. Obviously, it was too damn good," he replied, looking down at the mess he had made. They both laughed. They smiled and looked at each other until the burning pancakes pulled Asaya away. J ran off to wash up and wake Annette and JJ for breakfast.

Sitting at the table with her family made Asaya believe things were almost perfect, but she had a nagging feeling it was far from over. Mrs. Johnson had been away from home for almost a week and she missed her house, but it was also relaxing and peaceful to be in the middle of nowhere with her only daughter and her son-in-law, finally acting like they loved each other. She had always said turbulent times had a way of pushing people together. After breakfast, they all gathered in the living room area and turned on the television to watch Saturday morning cartoons with Little J. As they discussed the game plan, the Little Einsteins show was interrupted with breaking news from Seattle. The camera panned to a bullet-riddled car that both Asaya and James immediately recognized as Rey's. A reporter started speaking, "Police are on location as one man is killed in a hail of gunfire and another man is apprehended." The story ended with a picture of J.D. being taken into custody and the coroner taking away someone in a body bag from a scene surrounded in yellow tape.

Asaya sat there stunned; Rey was dead. After everything he had done, she should have felt relief, but she did not. Rey was out of the picture and they could go back home and live without looking over their shoulders, but it did not feel like all was well. She looked over at James and he seemed to be happy with the outcome. "Did you do this?" she asked angrily.

Taken aback by her ire, J looked at her and replied, "No, I didn't. They just showed who did it, but here you go pointing the finger at me!" Asaya looked away, not wanting her husband to know how upset she was.

"Funny... you so worried about the next man, but when you thought I ransacked your place, you wanted nothing to do with me. Just because your little boyfriend was a killer don't make me one, too!" He popped up from the couch and stormed out of the front door. Mrs. Johnson walked over to comfort Asaya, but she stood up and excused herself to go freshen up in the restroom.

As the warm water from the shower flowed over her body, she leaned against the wall and cried uncontrollably. Regardless of all the bad shit he had done, she had loved Rey ever since she could remember and it was hard to imagine never seeing him again. She thought about the years they spent together at Lakeside and the UW and even reminisced about the time in Hawaii. The love of her life was gone and she would never be the same again. J could get as mad as he wanted, but he and Asaya knew that when he was not around, which had been quite often, Rey was there to hold her down and make sure she and JJ were good. She stayed in the shower until the hot water was gone. When she finally exited the bathroom, J had returned and was no longer mad at her. He gave her a concerned look and walked over to comfort her, but Asaya pushed him away, letting him know his company was not needed or wanted. Annette held her daughter briefly before escorting her to the bedroom to rest.

THE RETURN

James Buchanan sat in the front pew at Christ the King listening to the Pastor preach. Today's scripture was based on Proverbs 17:9, "Love prospers when a fault is forgiven, but dwelling on it separates close friends." He looked down at his wife and son sitting next to him, and thanked God that they had overcome all the obstacles that were placed in front of them.

Initially, Asaya seemed to have a tough time functioning after Rey was killed, but eventually she started to go back to her normal self. She tried to hide that she was in mourning, but J could see the sorrow in her eyes. It would make him upset and he would need to keep himself from going off on her. He shook his head at the ignorance of being jealous of a dead man. He was not coming back and J would never have to worry about his wife's feelings for Rey again. Asaya returned her husband's gaze and gave him a weak smile. Ever since everything went down, he kept watching her like he was trying to read her mind or something. She had made the mistake of telling him she missed Rey once and he damn near lost his mind. She quickly learned to keep any thoughts on the subject hidden. It had been a little over a month since his death and she still thought about him every single day—sometimes all day. She wanted to go to his funeral, but J did not think it was the best idea, given all that had happened. She ended up watching the graveside ceremony from a distance anyway and putting flowers on top of his casket after the family left. She wanted to see him one last time, but his casket was closed due to the number of bullets he took and the damage to his face. She wanted to hug his mom and his sisters and tell them how sorry she was, but after they found out what James had done with For the People; they refused to speak to Asaya. The Pastor excused the congregation and the Buchanans socialized with everyone for a while before heading home.

James pulled up to their new condo near downtown Seattle. The house was still being rented out and they wanted a fresh start. Besides, he and Asaya felt more comfortable in the secure building. The garage could not even be entered without a security code. Although Rey was no longer a threat, J knew that he was a target because of his two thriving businesses. Nobody else he knew from the hood could say he had both a successful grocery store and legal medical marijuana grow operation. He had even found a new location for the Silver Spoon and inherited all of the fixtures and recipes that Will had accumulated. It was only a matter of time before the Buchanans were multi-millionaires. The living arrangements and social status were not the only things that had changed. After five years with the company, Asaya had decided to leave **Premier Finance and Accounting.** She was now James' accountant and business manager for all of his affairs. He had hoped to make her happy by giving her the position that paid ten times what she made slaving away in corporate America, but she still moped around from time to time. Mrs. Johnson told him that time heals all wounds. He hoped this one would heal quickly. James carried his son into the condo and laid him down in his bed. He then joined his wife on the couch for a movie. He had picked up a Key lime pie to surprise her with, because he knew it was her favorite. J disappeared into the kitchen and came out carrying two saucers with the delectable treats on them. When he sat Asaya's plate on the table, she just stared down at it as if it was the most disgusting sight she had ever seen. Before he could inquire, she jumped up and ran to the bathroom. He ran behind her to find her vomiting in the toilet. Over the past week, she had come down with the stomach flu. "I'm sorry, boo. I forgot you were sick," he said as he handed her a cold, wet washcloth to put on her face. J stood there with her until she finally stopped puking and walked her to the couch, before grabbing a pillow and blanket for her. As Asaya slept with her legs across his lap, he watched boxing reruns, thinking to himself, *Guess I won't be getting none tonight...*

Little J was really enjoying his new daycare and since his mommy and daddy worked together, he got to see both of them before and after work. Asaya bent down and gave her little man a hug and kiss. "I love you," she told him as she left. J opened the door for her and they got on I-5, headed out to the warehouse for the day. Their customer base was growing steadily and they were spending a lot more time making sure all I's were dotted.

They pulled up in front and Asaya waited for J to come around and open her door. "I could get used to this," she teased as he took her hand to help her out.

"You better," he smiled and pulled his lady in for a kiss.

Reyhan Lucas stood on his balcony watching the blissful couple through his telescope. He grimaced when he saw how lovey-dovey Asaya was with J, although she knew he had her *so- called* best friend killed. Obviously, she was not concerned with Rey; she hadn't even stopped by to see what was up with their old apartment and it was just a mile from her new workplace. He hadn't spotted her at the funeral either. Now she was helping her husband with the business he stole from Rey before trying to have him killed. Yes, this spot had been a good investment. When he found out that J had established a grow operation out in Woodinville on the down low, Rey immediately copped a location to post up and keep an eye on him, and his balcony gave him a bird's eye view. J was feeling himself and pretending to be the man, but Rey was an expert at giving the enemy just enough rope to hang himself.

BE SURE TO CHECK OUT PART 2

CPSIA information can be obtained
at www.ICGtesting.com
Printed in the USA
LVHW041705301020
670291LV00010B/1067

9 781507 685549